W9-DDO-212

WILDERNESS BRIDE

Books by Annabel and Edgar Johnson

THE BLACK SYMBOL

TORRIE

THE BEARCAT

THE RESCUED HEART

PICKPOCKET RUN

WILDERNESS BRIDE

by Annabel & Edgar Johnson

Harper & Row, Publishers
New York and Evanston

WILDERNESS BRIDE

Copyright © 1962 by Annabell J. and Edgar R. Johnson
Printed in the United States of America
All rights reserved. No part of the book may be used or reproduced in any manner whatsoever without written permission except in the case of brief quotations embodied in critical articles and reviews. For information address Harper & Row, Publishers, Incorporated, 49 East 33rd Street, New York 16, N.Y.

FIRST EDITION

G-M

Library of Congress catalog card number: 62-14603

For Margaret and Clyde Tallman

It was a star-crossed year—1846—that brought the crash of cannon along the southern border. The United States was at war with its neighbor, Mexico. And, to the north, another kind of gunfire spattered the darkness as mobs rode by night to burn the houses of their personal neighbors. The state of Illinois was waging a private war upon one of its own cities, a town called Nauvoo. Twenty thousand people were put to flight that year—driven westward, though where and how far they would go no one knew. One of them was a girl named Corey. . . .

PART ONE

One

It was almighty quiet. The woods lay under a morning hush and out across the fields heat waves rippled the still air. Over north a thread of dust hung, treetop high.

From the doorway of the cabin Corey watched it, arms tight at her sides, hands knotted hard. Then she turned and went back inside, her bare feet almost noiseless on the earthen floor. The stillness of the single barren room seemed to ring in her ears. Or was it the pound of her own heart? The echo of the hard words that Pa had spoken just now?

"You'll do as I say . . . I'll not have any back talk!" Angry and troubled—but his mind was made up. Corey shuddered.

It had all come on so suddenly. After these years of living here alone on the verge of the forest, just the two of them, easy and friendly, everything was finished. All their closeness was knocked to the four winds. In a day or so he would be heading one way and she, another—maybe never to see each other again. And this—because a man they'd never met had ordered it.

"It's not for us to question!" Pa had warned her sternly. "Brigham Young is head of the Church and the Lord's own apostle. What he directs, we must do. You're a mite headstrong to accept a command, especially when it's a hard one, but you'll learn. That's exactly why I got to make sure you're bound over to somebody who'll take care of you proper." His jaw was set, stubborn as a stone wall. "There'll be plenty of families camped at Sugar Creek—I hear that more'n a hundred came across the river just this week. I'll make out to place you with a good 'un."

But there was no time to waste in going back over the scene. By now he'd be a mile on his way. Hastily, Corey stripped off her patched homespun pants and put on her best pair of breeches, belting them in tight at the slender waist and tucking the shirt well down inside. Pouring water into the basin, she washed her hands, splashed some on her face, and slicked back the short locks of light sun-streaked hair.

She knew she was hardly togged out fit for a visit to a holy man, but she had to get somebody's advice—someone she could trust. She looked down at herself, frowning. The young face with its strong planes and native humor grew suddenly anxious, as she tried to remember those company manners her mother had taught her so long ago.

The shoes! Of course. From a corner she rummaged out a pair of heavy old boots and wiped the dust from them. No use trying to bring a gloss to the scuffed toes. She just hoped the Elder would understand how it was hard on leather, to work in corn stubble and tramp through briar thickets. Pulling them on, she started for the door; then another thought halted her.

On impulse she went over to her father's bunk and felt in the straw under the mattress. Nothing there. Puzzled, she flipped it back to look, but the old Black Hawk pistol was gone. He must have taken it with him, and likely for good reason, what with the woods full of Missourians these days, but right now she wished he had left it for her. She thought she might even be needing it worse than he did.

As she stepped out of the cabin into the clearing, she found the day already growing hot. Corn would be ripening fast now. Heading across the field at a long-legged stride, she thought it seemed a shame to go off and leave good grain, so near to harvest. But Pa said there was no time to wait for that. No time for anything. A little desperately she wondered, *why must everyone be in such a rush, such a fright?* The earth lay calm enough. Even old Mississip' looked lazy on a hot summer day.

Pausing on the riverbank, beside a small landing where a skiff was tied, she stared uneasily across the muddy sweep of water. Over there on the east shore stood the city—a shining, mysterious city. Nauvoo. In some ancient, sacred language the word was supposed to mean "beautiful," and it was. Rising in rows upon the hillside, where the river made a great bend, the ranks of gracious-looking houses shimmered under the sun. On the crest of the hill, the Temple stood above all the rest, bright light splintering off its golden spire. To Corey it had always looked somewhat the way she had privately imagined heaven.

The one time she had been there had left her with an awesome memory. A year ago, it was, when Pa had taken her to be baptized. She would never forget the shadowy inner room of the Sanctuary, with the huge marble basin supported by twelve giant carved stone oxen. She had been led into it, all garbed in a long, loose white robe, the icy water rising around her ankles, then her knees, step by step. And all the while the old men—the Elders—stood about, taller than natural.

It was one of these she must find now. Bracing against the little stir of fear which came inside her, Corey untied the skiff and stepped aboard, taking the oars briskly as the current grabbed the boat. Out here in the channel the water looked less placid, the face of the river was aboil with hidden undercurrents. Leaning back with a strong pull, she felt the blades dig in, the little boat thrust through the water.

She hadn't realized quite what a long haul it was. By the time she got to the opposite shore she was breathing hard, the hair plastered awry across her forehead. With one last drive she sent the bow up onto a pebbly beach and skipped over the side to draw the skiff up, high and dry.

And now she wished even more that she had Pa's gun, for there was a feel of danger in the air. No wagons to be seen on the road as she climbed the hill toward the city. And when she reached its streets, there wasn't a carriage in sight. The outskirts of town were quiet as a painted picture. No dogs barked from the empty yards—no one rocked on the porches. Blinds were drawn, doors padlocked. The stately buildings—solid brick and two stories high—stood eyeless and still. But this was no comfortable silence of the forest. Corey felt the perspiration break out and run down the nape of her neck.

Have they all gone? All—so soon? Of course she knew that during these past months thousands of people had crossed the river in desperate haste with whatever goods they could gather together. From the bluffs near home she had watched the barges coming, loaded with wagons and cattle—all bound first for Sugar Creek, where they organized into trains to go on westward. Yet she hadn't pictured the city as completely deserted!

And then, ahead, on a street corner, she saw another live person in this graveyard of a town—a girl, standing there blankly, holding a child by the hand. Not going anywhere, just standing. In a rush of relief, Corey crossed to her side with a little salute of greeting.

"Excuse me, ma'am, but I'm from across the river—I don't know my way around town. I'm wondering where I might find—"

"They came last night," the girl said, staring at her starkly. "There was thirty or more. I hid up in the attic, but I watched through a crack. They tore open the mattress and threw the feathers around. Said they was going to tar and feather us if they could find us. Baby wanted to cry—I near choked him, keeping him quiet."

"Who came?" Corey asked, with a small shiver. "Who was it? The mob?"

The girl hardly seemed to see her for all that wide-eyed look. "All been drinking spirits. Sinful drunk, they was. Swearing terrible. I can't go back there, they might come again."

"Do they ever come by day?" Corey glanced around uncomfortably.

"We ought to been gone from here," the girl went on tonelessly. "But the Council told my man he must stay. He has to help build more wagons. Always more wagons."

Corey made a little bow and said, "Well, good luck to you," and went on. No point in trying to make her listen. Pa had spoken of this once, what a terror a mob could spread. He'd seen plenty of them in Missouri ten years ago. Brutal, dirty crowds who thought it sport to beat a man, burn down a barn or tear up an orchard.

But why? she'd asked him, shocked.

Pa's face had taken on a shine of pride. "Because

we're Mormons, Corey. We're Latter-day Saints—the only people on earth who've been chosen by the Lord to sit in the highest place in heaven come Judgment Day. That makes the poor gentiles fret, they got to torment us. But you can forgive 'em, seeing they'll all have to burn in hell."

Corey wasn't so sure she could feel that generous if they had driven her out of one of these handsome homes. And she had heard what they could do to a woman—

Above the rooftops the spire of the Temple rose like a beacon; Corey headed for it. Once as she hurried along she thought she caught sight of a face at an upstairs window of one of the closed houses, but it was gone quickly. Past closed shops, empty stores with their goods still stacked on the shelves, she kept going, though the sight of a pretty array of hats in the milliner's window brought a grim quirk to her lips. Little veils and velvet flowers—the ladies wouldn't be needing those when they headed out across the wild country west of here.

As she came out into the square she slowed a moment, to approach the Temple cautiously, respectfully. And then she heard curiously earthy sounds coming from inside. The big doors were ajar. Looking in, she stared at the transformation. It had been turned into a wagoner's shop. Amid a clutter of lumber and flying chips from the workmen's axes sweating men hurried to set the tongue and crosstree of a half-finished wagon. Others pounded the last sideboards into place. The sound of hammers was drowned by the ring of the anvil—smiths at work, shaping the iron tires for the wheels that lay nearby.

The feverish pace at which they all labored made Corey hesitate to bother them with questions. As she walked over slowly, one of the men looked up from his work.

"The Elder?" he repeated. "Down there." Briefly he pointed to a corridor and swung his sledge again.

Corey paused a moment more, then blurted out the question. "Why must you make more wagons if everybody has gone?"

He glanced at her again grimly. "Gone? I wish they had. There's people—too many people—behind those locked doors."

As he went on with his work, she swallowed a new tremor of fear and went on toward the hallway he had indicated. It was dimly lit. At the far end she saw a door over which was posted a roughly lettered sign: PROPERTY FOR SALE. The Elder was seated at the desk inside, tallying figures in an account book. As Corey paused in the doorway he glanced up distractedly.

"What is it, lad?" Then he took a second look. "Mercy, child! I scarcely knew you! It's Judd Tremaine's girl, isn't it?"

"Yes, sir," she stammered, then went suddenly tongue-tied. For all he had ink smudges on his cuffs and his bald head was beaded with perspiration, this was one of the holiest men in the Church, who had seen visions and had even known the Prophet, Joseph Smith, personally. It was this Elder who had converted Pa to the faith, years and years ago.

"Sit down, my dear," he was saying kindly. "Is your father with you?"

"No, sir," Corey whispered. "It's about him that I've come to see you. Yesterday he was given an order from Brigham Young that he must go off and help fight a war against Mexico somewhere!" She flung out a hand in a nervous gesture.

"Ah, yes. I had heard that a battalion of Saints was being formed. Ironical that we must go and do battle for the very country which is allowing one of its states to drive us from our homes. Don't try to fathom it, child." The old man rubbed his brow wearily. "I can assure you that Brother Brigham has his reasons. Whatever he and the Council of Apostles order, your father must do."

"Oh, he means to." She nodded miserably. "But what I need to know, sir—would it be so awfully wrong for me to go, too? Pa says I mayn't, but sometimes he gets his mind set and won't listen to reason, so I thought I'd come to you."

The Elder regarded her fondly. "Your father knows that the army is no place for a young girl."

"But I can march and shoot and sleep out on the ground as well as any boy!"

The old man glanced at her clothes. "How long has your poor mother been departed, my dear?"

"I don't remember–it's been eight or nine years."
"And how old are you now?"

"Fifteen, almost. And I'm strong and fit. At least if I can't go with him, would it be so wrong for me to stay on our land and work it?"

The Elder's face took on a distant look. "Our future lies to the west, my child. The Scriptures say we must go forth into the wilderness and find a new land which will be called Zion. Out of the desert we will bring a garden of richness fit for the Lord's chosen people. You don't want to stay back here and forsake this great prophecy, now do you?"

"Well, of course I'd want to go there–later. But right now–well, we've got crops near ready to bring in. Everybody says food's needed almighty bad."

The Elder smiled a little. "Your father is probably planning some gentler future for you, fitting for a girl who's almost a woman grown."

"That's the whole trouble!" she blurted out. "He keeps saying I must be wed! Right now he's gone to Sugar Creek to search out some man who'll have me in marriage. Elder, *must* I do it? Pa's told me to make up my mind to it, but if you were to say the word–"

The Elder was shaking his head slowly. "It's in the Scriptures that you must honor your father. Also, that the holy state of matrimony is the only way a woman can attain grace and enter the blessings of heaven. Your father is a sensible man, I'm sure he'll make a wise decision."

"But I don't *want* to marry some stranger, to be his wife and have to do what he says!" she pleaded.

The Elder eyed her severely. "Want? You speak of what you 'want,' young lady, when the fires of hell are burning at our doorstep? We were persecuted in Independence thirteen years ago—our lands raped and our Temple desecrated. When we built new homes in Daviess County we were hounded from them, too, and our Prophet imprisoned. We came to this place and raised a new temple unto the Lord and now we must leave it—our Prophet is murdered and we are again driven forth. Here's a man"—he tapped the account book with his quill pen—"he's sold his house and orchard for a team of oxen. Do you suppose he *wanted* to?" He picked up a worn copy of the Book of Mormon which lay before him. "It has been written that the Lord wants a *tried* people. He sends us these ordeals to test our courage. Will you fail Him?"

"But marrying is so—so—permanent!"

"Dying is more so, child." Suddenly the Elder's tones sounded thunderous in the small room. "Your place in heaven—or hell—is for all eternity. Go home and do as your father bids."

Two

By the flickering light of the hearth fire Corey sighted down the barrel of the Black Hawk pistol, then rammed an oily rag through, pulling it out with a resentful jerk that made her father glance over at her anxiously.

"I don't see," she muttered, "why this battalion you're joining doesn't stay right here and fight the Illinois people. You could hold onto Nauvoo, and we all wouldn't have to go running off to the end of nowhere—"

"Corey!" he cut in quickly. "You're talking foolish." Pa was a sober man with earnest china-blue eyes that could punish you with reproach. The very longness of his face, with the blond hair combed neatly across the high forehead, lent a gravity to his displeasure. "I know you're all a-fluster over things, but you mustn't question the counsel of the Church—not even in a fit of temper. I'm going to Mexico, and you're going with Dan Tanner's family, and you'd best be composing yourself to accept it like a true saint."

Corey started to mention that she hardly felt like a saint but checked the thought. It was probably sinful, and anyhow it was too late to protest. She was defeated. Pa had made the arrangements and tomorrow she would be bound to this Dan Tanner's son. She hadn't even the heart to ask questions about him. After all, what kind of boy would consent to marry a girl he'd never seen? Unless— A sudden thought occurred to her.

"Pa, did Mr. Tanner force his son into this?"

He shook his head. "I'd not have gone along with that. Two colts fighting one rope is a bad business. No, I put the problem to them, and the boy was willing."

Slowly Corey asked, "What's he like?"

Her father didn't answer at once, suddenly becoming intent on the boot he was mending. At last he said, "Ethan's some different from the others. He's no blood kin to them—he's Tanner's stepson and was raised in England. Tanner met his ma there and married her last year on a preaching mission. So the boy speaks some different from us, but he's manly and decent. You can tell he's been well taught. It's good for a fellow to have schooling—I wish I had more."

"What does he look like?"

"Looks?" Pa eyed her sternly. "That's a frivolous thing to ask. You judge a man by his mind and hands and heart. All I say is, I'm satisfied. You've got into a good family, and I can go off to war knowing that if anything happens to me, you'll be taken care of. Tanner's as well off as any man I saw at Sugar Creek. He's the captain of the camp—the Council has stationed him there to help the others get on their way, fixing up their wagons and the like. He's a carpenter by trade, and high in the Church—he's a deacon. A kindhearted man, too. It's not everybody would take another girl into his family right now with times so hard, and even be willing to keep her like a daughter till she's turned sixteen and can be wed."

Corey wheeled around to face him, hardly able to believe what she'd just heard. "You mean I'm not to be married for a year yet!"

"Certainly not. I'd never let you be sealed to a man before you were of a good age. Besides," Pa went on, frowning, "you've much to learn. It worries me some. I tried to do my best by you, but you've led a wayward life, without any woman to keep discipline over you. I don't regret that you know how to shoot a gun and swing an axe, but there's a whole world of other things you'll have to learn before you'll make a wife. Mainly, you've got to set yourself to obey the counsel of the Church and live by the word of the Bible, no matter what comes." He knotted his thread and broke it off.

Corey finished cleaning the pistol and laid it beside his pack. "I thought the Bible says you shalt not kill."

Pa glanced up frowning. "That don't include things

like wars. There were all sorts of wars in the Bible. I can see you are short on faith, and it's my fault. I should've explained more of it to you. Then you could accept it all better. Because these things we're going through were all set down in the Scriptures—writ on plates of pure gold!" His blue eyes stretched wide with awe at the thought. "Can you imagine what that means, Corey? Just like in olden days, we had a prophet of our very own, come to earth on purpose to teach us. You'll hear the disbelievers—the gentiles—you'll hear 'em say Joseph Smith was just a plain man, but the evidence proves different!" He smacked his fist into his palm. "First he found a passel of golden plates where they'd lain buried over the ages, and then on top of that he had a vision to let him translate the secret symbols and signs engraved on 'em. It's nigh as fearsome as Moses bringing down the Commandments. Fact, it *is* as fearsome. Off those plates we got our own whole book of the Bible—and don't ever let anybody tell you the Book of Mormon ain't true Scripture. So I say, it's no common man done all that."

Corey had heard the story often enough—there were a few things about it that bothered her. And since the Church was taking a hand in her own future she thought she must ask, even though it should rile Pa.

"I wonder," she ventured, "why do you reckon the golden plates said our Temple should be built in Missouri, yet we got run out of there, and run out of here, too?"

Pa stared at her indignantly. "There's nothing in Scripture says the Lord can't change His mind!"

That relieved her considerably, because if one thing could change, so could another, and a year is a long time. Anything might happen—

"This that we're instructed to do now," Pa was going on in a sort of fixed rapture, "is the greatest command ever given to us: To go forth and find a new Zion in the West—maybe have to go as far as Californy or Oregon or some other heathen place. It'll be a long trip full of danger and suffering, which you must take patiently, like a true saint, and at the end there'll be a fair land where no man has ever stepped before, so far away from the cursed gentiles they'll never be able to come at us again. That's where you're going, Corey! And that's where I'll come, too, when our service in the war is over. All the saints on earth will be there someday, and we'll live according to the Bible, just as things were in ancient times. Even if some of the old laws do seem strange. . . ."

All at once the excitement in his voice became mixed with uncertainty, as if he were searching for a hold on a slippery chunk of rock. "Yes, sir, we got to accept some curious commandments, Corey, and that's where faith comes in. You feel like you got a little more faith, now?"

"I reckon," she said uneasily, sensing something else to come, some further calamity.

"Then I better tell you about the rest of Dan Tanner's household," he went on. "No need to be startled

—you've heard these things whispered and so have I, though I never knew for sure that they was true."

"That what was true?"

Pa looked at her solemnly. "You know it's been said that some men of favor in the Church have been given —in spirit anyhow—more than one wife?" He took a deep breath. "Dan Tanner has three."

All night Corey had thought about heaven and hell and three mothers-by-marriage instead of one; she'd thought about the knuckling under she was going to have to do; the terrible moment when she was going to have to face this boy, Ethan, and look at him pleasantly. She had thought of Pa and war and death. But next morning, as they started out, all she could think of was how gawky she looked.

Skirts pulled up to her knees, dangling long legs sheathed in white stockings, she rode her mare astraddle, as a horse should be ridden, but it made a comic picture. Even old Peggy thought so and kept swinging her head around to sniff at the silly, narrow button shoes on Corey's feet—hot, woman-style shoes as foolish as all the rest of these trappings. Petticoats, bodices, and the blousy calico dress, which was tied up tight around her throat like a flour sack. It was a poor fit—the woman Pa had bought the clothes from had been a good deal bigger in front. The worst of it was, Corey didn't know how to handle herself. For the first time in her life she felt clumsy.

"We're almost there," Pa said, out of a mile-long

silence. His black flat-crowned hat was set squarer than usual, and beneath the straight brim he was stony-faced, nearly as miserable as she was. "Maybe you better start riding like a lady."

Corey swung her foot over to perch sideways on the mare's back and pulled her skirts down with such a flap, Pa's horse jumped three feet off the trail.

"Ho, now, ho." He quieted the animal, and to Corey he added, "You remember your manners! And be extra polite to Sister Trude. She's Tanner's first wife and has the say-so over the household."

Corey nodded gloomily. She had already supposed that someone must give the orders in a big family like that. Everybody knew that women can't ever agree. What could be worse than a whole flock of them, all bickering over what to have for dinner or who should wash the dishes? She had heard, before, of this "spiritual marriage"—it was even rumored that this was one of the reasons the Illinois were determined to run the Mormons out. But she had never pictured herself as being touched by it. Now it was coming into new proportions.

As they rode into the outskirts of the encampment, it was hardly a sight to lift the spirits. A hodgepodge of tents and wagons and makeshift shelters; some families didn't even have a piece of canvas to stretch over the little piles of tumbled bedding that lay on the ground. Of course, one reason everything was so disorganized was that this was the first place people headed after they landed on the Iowa shore. The camp had been set up eight miles inland from the river, to discourage the Illinois marauders from coming across and raiding, and even that short trip was difficult for people who had just taken the trail for the first time.

Some wagons had broken down—the older ones were coming apart at the seams under too-heavy loads. There was obviously plenty of need for carpenters such as Tanner. Even now a dozen or more swaying, creaking, rickety old boxes, just arrived, were milling through the grounds as their owners looked for places to camp. Dust rose in clouds on the air, mixed with the choking stench of ox dung and the blue haze of wood smoke from a hundred campfires. And the noise was chaos. Oxen bawled, horses nickered, children yelled. Corey felt a lump of fright in the pit of her stomach. *How does anyone live in the midst of all this?*

"Here's Tanner's camp," Pa said.

It was a spacious site bordered by shade trees. Four big canvas-topped wagons and other smaller equipment made a semicircle around a large central fireplace, where a leg of pork was being turned on a spit by a scowly little boy. At the big table beyond, the women and girls were at work preparing a meal. Over to one side two men were trying to repair a huge broken-down freight wagon. The big one with the flowing black beard must be Tanner, Corey supposed—he was shaping a new axle out of an oak log, swinging the hatchet expertly. The younger one was working to take off the wheel. A boy of eighteen or so, he was muscular and sturdy, with a start on a short brown beard of his own.

"Is that the one, Pa?" she whispered.

"No." He swung off his horse and held up a hand to help her down. "That's Tanner's other stepson—his second wife's boy."

Tanner saw them now and laid his work aside. "So here y'are, Tremaine," he called in a resounding voice that would have carried clear to the Mississippi. "You've brought the lass, eh? Let's have a look at her."

The women left their work, too, and all of them gathered around, sizing Corey up and down, the way they would a filly on the auction block. She was trembling with rebellion, but managed to meet their stares unflinching.

Tanner nodded approvingly. "She's a bold one, to look a body in the eye like that. She'll be good for Ethan. Sarah, go call the boy, tell him his bride's here." One of the younger girls skipped away, beaming with some mysterious mirth. Meanwhile, Dan was going on with introductions.

". . . Sister Trude . . ." A gaunt, unsmiling woman with a bun of gray hair held in place by big jet-black pins. She kept plucking at Corey's dress, as if to try to bring some fit into it, but Corey thought she was also trying to judge how strong an arm lay under the loose sleeve.

". . . Sister Millie . . ." A brown-haired dimpled

woman with soft brown eyes that were warm and friendly. The husky young man, Shad, was her son, and most of the younger children were hers, too, although Corey lost track of the names in all the confusion.

"And Sister Elizabeth is kept to her wagon just now," Tanner finished. "She's under the weather. You'll meet her later. But here comes her boy, anyway. Hurry along, Ethan!"

Corey's first thought was: *he's tall enough!* Lean, but well built. And then she realized there was something strange about him. The clothes must be of foreign cut and cloth—they weren't exactly American, anyhow. But the difference went deeper than that. As he came up, he took off his hat in a quaint gesture of courtesy. A slender, clean-shaven face, it was too tight. The dark eyes were shadowed by some trouble that gave a somber cast to his expression. And yet he was young. There was a boyishness in the way he shoved the loose dark hair back off his brow, murmuring an apology for having kept them waiting.

"Well, well, boy," Tanner spoke impatiently, "it's no compliment to your bride. Here she is—Miss Corinne Tremaine. Give her a proper greeting, now!"

Ethan turned to Corey with a swift, questioning appraisal. She shoved out a hand to shake, but he took it lightly, turned it over so that the freckles on the back showed. With a little bow he said in a low voice, "Your servant, Miss Tremaine."

"That's British," Tanner explained, "for saying 'glad to meet you.' Ethan's not grown to our ways yet, but he'll learn." He slapped the boy on the shoulder. "You'll make a fine-looking pair, good straight grain in both of you, even if you do need a bit of shaping around the edges." He was eying Corey's short locks. "Sister Millie, lend me your sunbonnet." Taking the floppy thing, he settled it on Corey's head. "That's better. Keep it on, daughter, till your hair grows to a proper length. And you, boy, put your hat on, too. You look foolish. Now then, the bridal pair is ready to grace the table."

It took Corey a few seconds to realize that the reason Ethan was holding out his elbow was that he expected her to hook a hand through it. Shyly she accepted the offer and even tried to muster a weak smile, but he seemed hardly to notice. Corey had the curious feeling that after the first moment's reckoning his mind had strayed away in some other direction.

The older women had gone to the fire to bring food to the table, but now Tanner stopped them. "Let it stay where it is a minute, Sisters. Everybody gather around. We'll hear these two say their vows first."

Pa—! Corey looked at him in consternation. *You never told me about this part!*

He returned the glance with a slight frown that said, Go on with it.

She swallowed hard. It hadn't been her intention to make any promises if she could help it, but Dan was confronting the two of them now, both hands raised in a mighty gesture.

"We're here to witness a betrothal, Lord!" he roared heavenward. "These children aim to enter your most blessed state. Help 'em bear up and be ready for it, seeing it ain't easy, what lies ahead of us. And meanwhile, help 'em keep these vows they're going to take." Lowering his look to Ethan, he went on almost warningly, "You, son, you'll take good care of this girl, treat her with respect till you're sealed in marriage, and cherish her ever after—that means you'll have to pitch in and work. Provide her with board and shelter and accept the responsibilities for her and the family you'll get. You ready to swear to this?"

Some overtone in the words had brought a slight rise of color to Ethan's face, but he answered steadily, "I swear it."

Dan turned to Corey. "And you, daughter, you'll be dutiful and true, hold yourself faithful to this man until you be sealed to him, and make a good wife afterward, accepting the lean times with the fat, the faults with the virtues, giving him comfort and stiffening his spirits if he lags. You swear this?"

Corey took a long, shaky breath. Tremulously she repeated, "I swear."

Three

To Corey it was the longest meal ever held. While the rest of them were expressing admiration for the fine language of the betrothal vows, which Dan admitted with modest satisfaction he had just made up on the turn of the moment, she sat silent beside Ethan, trying to rally some show of appetite, though her stomach felt as if a bird had got loose in it.

It had been a long time since she had practiced polite table manners. Out of the corner of her eye she watched Ethan cut his meat and tried to get the hang of holding the fork right, though she still couldn't see the sense of blunting a good knife blade against a china plate. She and Pa had wooden trenchers at home.

And then the talk turned in her direction and she had to juggle the steaming dishes of food—potatoes and stewed apples and greens—while at the same time she balanced the answer to some question.

"I s'pose you're right good at quilting?" Sister Trude had asked.

"Never tried it, ma'am," Corey answered, struggling to pass the big bowl of gravy, which would have capsized if Ethan hadn't come quickly to her assistance.

"I'll be mighty happy to show you some patterns," Sister Millie was offering. "You'll be needing quilts. They say the nights are fearsome cold out where we're going, across the high mountains."

"There's better ways to warm a bed than quilts," Shad had commented, with a swift wink at Corey. She lowered her eyes in confusion. Millie began to cluck, but he went on innocently. "Such as wool blankets. Do you weave, Sister Corey?"

"How long do you bake your bread?" Sister Trude again.

Corey looked straight across at her. "We always fried ours, ma'am. I reckon there's not much I know about your kind of housekeeping, but I learn fast."

"Sure she does," Pa put in stanchly. "I never seen anybody pick up the tricks of plowing as quick as she did."

Shad choked on a mouthful of mashed potatoes, and both Trude and Millie were about to speak, when Dan Tanner slammed a fist on the table so hard the dishes jumped.

"And the day may come when we get to Zion that a woman will have to take a hand in the fields. A good thing, to know all the skills you can. Now you ladies hush your clapperjaw. I want to talk to Tremaine about this battalion. I swear, I'm not too glad we're losing five hundred of our best men, right now when we need every hand to get us westward, though I reckon Brother Brigham knows what he's doing."

"Our army pay will be sent back to the Church," Pa explained, "to be used to help you and the others get a new city started. So we'll be doing our part in settling the promised land."

As the talk veered away from her, Corey tried to force down a little food, but it wasn't easy. She noticed that Ethan had hardly touched his, either. He kept glancing over his shoulder toward the one wagon which was set farthest from the fire. Once, when he turned back and caught Corey watching him, she whispered cautiously.

"Is your mother very sick?"

He hesitated; she glimpsed some mixture of emotions in his look. At last he said, "It comes and goes. She may be quite recovered when we visit her. In fact, I wish you might pretend that she isn't ill at all—if you can manage that."

"Of course, if you say so," she agreed, puzzled.

"You're quite—forthright," he added uncertainly. "Do you really think you can dissimulate?"

"I reckon I can do whatever you show me how to do, long as it's not some sin!" With rising defiance Corey was about to pursue the matter, but the dinner was breaking up now. Pa had said he must be on his way, and all at once her own personal grief flooded in on her, engulfing everything else.

They had to say their good-bys in front of all the others, as stiff and formal as if they were strangers, though the wordless question was crying, louder than ever, inside her.

Why did you choose this one, Pa?

"Be a good girl." He patted her shoulder affectionately and turned away to mount his horse.

As he rode off through the late-afternoon haze, it was as if all the world she'd ever known was drifting away. Who would ever again be as close—listen to her ideas, even when they were silly? Or laugh at the same things she did? Who'd ever take her fishing—! Corey felt weak and lost.

A light touch on her arm brought her back to find Ethan at her side. "Are you all right? Do you feel faint? I can get you some smelling salts."

A rush of resentment helped steady her. "I am certainly not faint!" she retorted hotly. "I'm not a vaporish sort of woman!"

"That's fortunate," he commented gravely. "I know this is all difficult for you, but I wanted to say that you needn't be afraid I'll make your life harder—"

"I'm not afraid of you or anyone else!" she cried furiously. "But don't try to turn me different than I am! Leastways, not yet! If I'm—'forthright'—then it's my nature. In a year I reckon you'll have the right to order me to be anything you say, but meantime, please leave me alone!" The outburst startled her as much as it did him—all the frustration she'd felt for two days pouring out in a torrent of panicky words. Corey bit her tongue and wished she could have taken it all back. For the wariness in his face had deepened.

"I'll take you to meet my mother now," he said. "Please act in any way you see fit."

Sick at heart, Corey tried to summon words to apologize. She felt an awful impulse to bolt off into the woods, run far and fast, away from this whole lot. And yet she let him lead her across the yard, and tried to brace herself for one more ordeal. Nor did it help much to hear one of the littler children whisper to another.

"Is she going to live in *that* wagon?"

She wasn't long in finding out the reason for that awed question. As she ducked under the back flap of canvas which Ethan held, she found herself in a different world. The world of England, set down in Iowa. The wagon was crowded with beautiful furnishings: tapestries hung from the canvas top to make walls within walls; there was a square of rich carpeting underfoot and the pervading sweetness of scented candles, which burned in silver sconces. It was all unreal as a dream.

On every side were china figurines of huntsmen and shepherdessess—and as delicate as any of them was the little woman who sat, clad in a filmy boudoir gown, framed by her elegant little bed—an exquisite piece of furniture that almost filled the front of the wagon, its delicate carved canopy hung with silken curtains. She leaned back against embroidered pillows, as white and perfect as porcelain, a finger marking her place in the book which lay in her lap. As she saw Corey she smiled—an innocent, radiant greeting.

"Is this the dear child?"

It came over Corey that she ought to drop a curtsey—something about Sister Elizabeth seemed to require it—and she made an awkward little bob. The doll-like woman was delighted. Ethan seemed surprised, but made no comment as he set down Corey's leather trunk beside the narrow trundle bed that was crowded into one back corner of the wagon. Then he motioned her to go forward.

"Did you tell me that you met her in London, Ethan?" Sister Elizabeth asked uncertainly.

"No, Mother. In Nauvoo. We met at church six months ago."

Bitterly Corey wondered if Pa knew that he had promised her to a first-rate liar.

"Oh, yes." His mother was smiling. "I remember now. Mr. Tanner is a friend of her family, you said."

"Of her father." Ethan nodded.

"You've no mother, dear?" Sister Elizabeth's dark eyes grew soft with sympathy. "Well, you shall have from now on. We'll have such fun, dressing you in something that becomes you—oh, we'll make you a lovely gown! A dark one, I think—blue, to match your eyes? What color is your hair, dear? Do take off your bonnet."

It was all put so graciously, with such genuine kindness that the tight coils of resistance began to uncurl inside Corey as she undid the sunbonnet.

"Oh, lovely! You're light-haired. Come here, child, sit closer." She beckoned Corey over to sit on the footstool beside the bed, and put out a hand—such a perfect little hand—to lift the short locks, making an experimental curl around one finger, her head tipped to one side like a bright-eyed little hummingbird. "Very nice. It's going to look very nice! Oh, I'm so glad you've come to us!"

All at once, for no reason, a mist of tears blurred Corey's vision. She ducked her head, blinking them back furiously.

"Ethan," Sister Elizabeth said lightly, "leave us a while, son. We have things to talk of which are entirely outside the realm of masculine interest."

With some hesitation he murmured an assent. When he had gone, his mother reached out to stroke Corey's hair again.

"Go on and cry, child," she said softly. "We all must, when we see our young, free, careless days slip away."

Four

Of course there was a certain satisfaction in learning to make bread. That was bound to be useful, no matter what happened. Gingerly, Corey punched the risen dough and began to fold it over on itself, being careful not to spill flour on the table—Sister Trude was fierce about waste. As she began to work it intently, Corey was aware that someone had come up beside her to watch.

It was Meg, the younger of Trude's two daughters—a handsome girl in her own moody way, dark-haired and dark of look, with a temper that could scald. Now she was being languid and sweet.

"Did you notice," she said carelessly, "when we got the potatoes out for supper last night how the whole sackful is beginning to put out shoots? They'll soften up something dreadful if they're not sprouted. I just thought that's something you could do—when you're finished there, of course. No hurry."

This had been coming on the whole week since Corey had taken a place in the household—Meg, hinting and then suggesting and now ordering, though the two of them were about the same age. It seemed a good time to meet the test of wills head-on.

Corey looked up at her with a show of coolness. "That's a job the small fry can do. I've got better things to turn my hand to."

Meg's lips tightened, though she still spoke with exaggerated charm. "It's not your fault, Sister Corey, but you do have a deal to learn about camp life. We all share the work, and since there's so many things yet you *don't* know how to do, I think you'd better pitch in on what you can. Sloth is a sin."

"Conceit's a worse one, Sister," Corey retorted kindly. "Who made you my mistress?"

"I declare, Sister, you seem to forget you're the newest member of this family."

"And you seem to be under some fancy that I hired on as a servant girl. I have to remind you that I'm a promised wife and will take a place near the head of the table before you will, *Sister!*" By the rise of color in Meg's face, Corey knew she had touched a sensitive spot.

Furiously the girl laughed. "And a curious way to reach heaven, wed to a featherhead." She stalked off, skirts twitching, headed for Sister Trude's wagon.

Corey supposed there would be the devil to pay, now, but she didn't much care. Meg's last words rang in her ears like an echo of all her own doubts.

In these past few days it had become plainer at every turn that Ethan was a strange person in this time and place. Even the other members of the family were troubled about him, and with reason. At meals he made little effort to join in the general talk. Around the camp he was even more offish; when someone addressed him, his response was polite but short. The most embarrassing part to Corey, however, was the way he lagged at any kind of work.

If he was given a piece of carpentry to do, he was so slow at it that Dan usually took it away from him impatiently and finished it himself. When he was sent to bring in the stock at night, he'd be gone for an hour or more, even though the cattle and horses were all pastured together in a big fenced field. Sometimes Ethan could be seen just standing, leaning on the top rail of the fence, staring into space.

To Corey he had been courteous, but at times she glimpsed a watchfulness in his face that she thought was secretly critical. She knew she lacked all the natural graces of a gentlewoman like Sister Elizabeth. She was willing enough to try to acquire some of them, but when Ethan was around she seemed to freeze up and stammer, so that from the beginning she found herself trying to avoid him.

"Sister, you don't have to knead that dough so hard!"

It was Lucy, Trude's older daughter, an angular, rawboned girl in her mid-twenties. Her long, homely face was usually alight with some secret humor, but it was a kindly sort. Now she dropped an arm about Corey's shoulders with careless affection. "I know, you've got somebody wadded up there on the breadboard and you're wringing her neck. Didn't I see Meg over here a while ago?"

"I wasn't thinking of her," Corey protested.

"She's got a hard life," Lucy went on, mock-sober. "She has to look at me, growing older every day with no offers of marriage. Every time she reflects what a horrible fate it is to be a spinster, it gives her wasps in her petticoat."

Corey bit down on a smile. "Do you think this is ready to bake?"

"It looks fine." Lucy turned grave for a minute. "You're doing so well, Corey—don't let Meg belittle you. I never saw anyone learn things so quickly. I wish I had your knack."

"It's no trick." Corey stared at her, surprised. "You just have to take hold sometimes. I remember the first time I ever rowed a boat—I was just a little pitcher about Sammy's age. I was playing in our skiff when the rope came untied. I learned how to pull an oar pretty fast, what with old Miss' spreading out around me."

Lucy laughed. "I'm glad you're that sort. Maybe you can 'take hold' of Ethan, one of these days, and steer him out of the shallows. None of the rest of us have been able to." She looked across toward the big tent where Dan and the boys slept, then her look shifted to the wagon next to it. "Oh, dear, here comes Mama with the bell. Looks like we're in for a time. Notice the hairpins."

Sister Trude was striding across the camp, long skirts switching. Corey thought the jet-black pins really did seem to stick out more severely than usual. As she came she was ringing her little brass bell, the signal for the rest of the households to come join in a family meeting. Meg was following after, with a small satisfied smile. Corey braced herself for the worst.

In a matter of minutes they had all gathered about the table—everyone but Dan, who was off working in another part of the campground, and Sister Elizabeth, who never left her wagon. Although she never seemed actually ill, just the same each morning when she wakened she would remark that she was feeling somewhat tired and didn't believe she would dress for the day. Ethan took all her meals in to her—even now he was returning the breakfast dishes, which he set aside before taking his place next to Corey in the circle. Standing so close, she could feel a distinct current of resentment stiffening him, though his face was under strict control as he waited, respectfully, with the others to hear Sister Trude's pleasure.

She had seated herself at the head of the table with Millie on her right. The rest of them stood quietly while she studied a piece of paper she had before her, tapping smartly with her pencil as she scanned it. At last she looked up at them, frowning.

"Any day now," she began, "we'll be heading out along the trail, going to go two-three thousand miles, who knows? And we are not going to get there without a mort of effort—I mean common effort, everybody pitching in, right down to the youngest. This past week I've been keeping track of what each and every soul did, and it's not enough. It'll never get us through on a hard pull across the mountains."

As she paused, Sister Millie spoke up mildly. "I think they've been trying, Sister. Maybe they just need it set out plainer, what you want them to do."

"Which is what this meeting is for. We're going to even things up. My two girls"—Trude rapped the piece of paper with her knuckles—"spent over seventeen hours last week dishwashing, and helped with the cookery twelve. Millie, your whole lot never put in more than twenty-two hours around this fireplace—and that's the point, the common chores. What-all goes on in your own wagon you got to be judge of, yourself."

Millie nodded, but there was a trace of indignation in her voice as she said, "I won't make excuses—if my young'uns didn't do their share, they should, though you'll have to admit the baby's a mite small to be much help yet."

"Sammy's not—he's six years old," Trude came back firmly, "and all he's done is turn the spit. From now on he can sprout the potatoes."

Corey glanced at Meg, who returned the look with a wait-and-see-you'll-get-yours expression.

On and on Sister Trude went, detailing their various assignments, proceeding upward through the ranks of Millie's children, from Sammy to Sabritha, Staley, Samantha, Saul, and Sarah, who was twelve. They stood like stairsteps around the far end of the table, dark-headed like Dan, brown-eyed and plump, like Sister Millie; their faces were a picture of woe as the list of duties went on.

"Now, for the older girls." Sister Trude scanned her sheet. "They must be here at the fire one hour before supper to help with the cooking however the need rises. Special chores—baking will be done by Lucy, Corey to help. Meg will do the milking, Corey, the churning. As for the dishes, Lucy—wash, Meg—dry. Corey can scour the pots and pans—that includes kettles, skillets, and skewers." Sister Trude glanced at her sharply. "Unless you think that chore's too heavy for you, Miss? It's no child's work."

Corey smiled. "No, ma'am. I'll be glad to do it." A dirty job—a good, dirty job!

"As for the men . . ." Trude turned her page over and studied it.

"When it comes to the heavy work," Millie put in, "I swear I think that should count more than the light. Maybe it don't take a thousand hours a week to chop wood, but my Shad's done all of it, and it's bone-hard labor."

Shad looked virtuous and sober. "I was just thinking, if any of these young ladies would like to trade their hours for all them buckets of water I carry, I'll swap 'em, even-steven."

Meg turned on him tartly. "I'd like to see you have my duty—feeding your baby brother! I'd like to see your face the first time he hiccuped his dinner all over you."

Trude put in quickly: "Stop that squabbling, both of you! Young man, you keep a civil tongue—you're not overworked."

"No, ma'am," he agreed. "But I do get some bored with doing the same thing all the time. How about if I trade chores with Brother Ethan? Come to think of it, I don't know what his are."

For the first time Sister Trude looked uncomfortable. "Well, Ethan's had his ma to care for. But now there's Corey to help with that, I reckon it's only right if he takes on some regular camp duties." She looked over at him thoughtfully. "Suppose we say half the water. Shad fetch in the morning, Ethan, at night when Shad has to chop wood."

Ethan inclined his head in acceptance. "Do you want me to continue to bring the stock in?"

Trude nodded. "And I'll have to say, plain and simple, it's been taking too long. When we get on the trail, there'll be no time for daydreaming. We'll have more heavy work to do then, what with wagons to drive, make and break camp. Another thing—wherever we stop, it'll be up to you and Shad to dig the slop pits."

Ethan didn't answer; it seemed all he could do to nod.

Shad gazed up at the sky. "I can hardly wait," he murmured. "I mean—for us to get the word and start out looking for that promised land."

Five

Little stitches—a thousand prickly little stitches. And August had turned off hotter than usual. It always was a green, steamy month along the Mississippi—no kind of weather to sit indoors and sew a piece of velvet. A trickle of perspiration broke loose from the roots of Corey's hair and ran down her cheek—cautiously she swiped at it, stealing a glance at Sister Elizabeth.

It was unbelievable how cool and dainty she looked, sitting over there in her little bed, reading—always reading. She hardly seemed real in the midst of this earthy place, with the dust and racket and sweat of Sugar Creek campground going on just beyond the canvas walls of the wagon.

In here it was quiet and remote and almost unbearably hot. The pucker strings were always drawn tight —Sister Elizabeth had an aversion to insects, she said.

Corey thought she just plain didn't like to get mosquito-bit, and who did? But it meant they had to keep the candles lit all day, and aside from using a sinful lot of them, it made the place so close that Corey sometimes thought she couldn't draw another breath. She was just about to suggest they open the front curtain for a little air, when Sister Elizabeth looked up.

"Do you feel a draft, dear? I believe I do."

Corey laid her work aside and went to get the lacy shawl which always hung near the bed, helping to arrange it around her shoulders.

"Thank you, child. You're very kind." She smiled, and Corey forgave her the candles and stitches and everything else. "Do you read, my dear?" she was going on brightly.

"I know how," Corey admitted. Pa had only two books—the Bible and the Book of Mormon—but for a while he had made her read aloud, a chapter a day from one or the other. That was some time ago, though—she hoped she wouldn't have to prove it now.

"Poetry is such a solace," Sister Elizabeth mused dreamily. "I can't imagine how anyone lives without it. It takes your mind and flies away into such beautiful thoughts. I do hope you'll read poetry to Ethan later on, when you're together."

"Yes'm." Corey bent over her work again.

"I used to, but lately he doesn't seem to listen. And yet, a man needs it. They're too engrossed in their business affairs. You have to try to keep them from becoming grim. Don't you feel that Ethan is just the least bit grim?"

Carefully Corey said, "I reckon he's just thinking about the trip west. They say it's not going to be easy."

A trace of surprise shadowed her lovely face. "He's going to Wales? He didn't tell me that."

Corey dug in with her needle. She had noticed before that Sister Elizabeth seemed confused, sometimes, as to where she was.

"No, ma'am," she said. "More likely California."

"Where, did you say? California? Where is that, dear?"

"Out west of here somewhere—that's where we're all going one of these days, you know."

"All? We're all—?" Sister Elizabeth began to look alarmed. Outside the children were making a racket, playing some kind of game that sent them into shrieks of laughter. Sarah's voice rose stridently:

"Lucy, Lucy,
She's a goosey!"

And one of the others yelled:

"Meg, Meg,
Is a rotten egg!"

It was the kind of foolish sport that all small fry delight in, but it upset Sister Elizabeth. Glancing about distractedly, she put a hand to her head.

"Why don't their nannies make them behave?" she

cried, a little frantically. "Please—ask the cook to close the gate to the garden. They'll be trampling the roses."

Outside little Sammy was screeching:

"Shad, Shad,
He's real bad!"

"I'll put a stop to it—" Corey began, when Sarah shouted with new inspiration:

"Ethan, Ethan,
He's not breathin'."

Sister Elizabeth put both hands over her face. "Why don't they go away? Where's Dr. Drake? Please call Dr. Drake!"

Corey dumped the sewing out of her lap and hurried to the rear of the wagon, loosened the pucker string, and ducked out under the canvas flap. When the children saw her, they hushed and stood, giggling a little.

"Your mother would strip your bottoms for making fun of folks," she scolded gently. "Sister Elizabeth isn't feeling well, so all you little saints go down to the creek and pick berries or something."

"I don't want to be a saint," Sammy commented.

But now Sarah grew suddenly grave with self-importance. "You children are very naughty," she told the others loftily. "Come on away."

When Corey went back inside, she found Sister Elizabeth still bunched over, her face hidden in her hands. "There, now"—she put an arm around the trembling shoulders—"they've gone home. They didn't hurt the roses."

"Is Ethan here?" Sister Elizabeth asked faintly.

"You lie back and rest. I'll go find him." When she had got the frail little woman stretched out, Corey went back outside, pulling the string tight behind her. She felt as if she had aged a year in these last few minutes. Dr. Drake—? Some family friend, back in England? One thing, though, came clear enough: she knew now why it was that Ethan sometimes looked toward their wagon and forgot what he was doing. For the first time she could feel a sympathy for him. As she walked out across the barren camp, its sparse greenery so trodden under foot that only a few dusty blades of grass remained, she wondered what it would be like—to have a whole rose garden.

"Well, bless me if the bride ain't beginning to be as hoighty as the groom!" The cheerful voice startled her out of her thoughts. Shad was leaning on the axe, one foot cocked on the woodpile—he'd been about to start his chores. A length of log was set upright before him, but he seemed in no hurry to begin. Straightening up, he made a little bow in an imitation of Ethan's manner. "Sister Corey, wouldn't you do me the elegance to say 'Howdy'?"

This one, she thought, had been asking for a comeuppance for quite a while. She wished there were time to attend to it right now. Instead, she kept her temper and said, "Evening, Shad. I was looking for Ethan. Have you seen him?"

"Tell you the truth, I just don't hardly notice the little people around here, I got my nose so up in the air."

"Mockery's mean enough when it comes from the young'uns," she retorted sharply, "but yours has got fishhooks in it." She was starting past when Shad stepped forward to block her way.

"I always heard that a gal don't scold unless she likes a fellow."

"That's no proper thing to be supposing. You'd best get your mind on your work."

"And I say you're bluffing me. What girl wouldn't rather be courted by a man who can swing an axe?"

"There's no special virtue in that," she snapped. Stepping over to the log that was set up, she yanked the axe free, took a good solid grip and swung, with all the knack Pa had taught her. The blade struck the grain just right—the log lay split. Carelessly she shoved the axe into Shad's hands, but he was looking past her, startled and a little sheepish. Corey turned to see that Ethan had come up, carrying a bucket of water, and was watching them with a gravity that made her squirm with embarrassment.

"I was looking for you—" she faltered.

"So I notice," he said.

"She was that, for sure," Shad put in, his bravado coming back fast. "I stopped her—I needed a lesson in how to split firewood. Handy gal you've got, Brother. She'll be useful if you ever need a little blaze to thaw you out—come a cold day, I mean."

"It will be a cold day—in Hades—when I require you to instruct me in my wife's abilities," Ethan said curtly, and walked on toward the center of camp. Corey followed after, smarting.

"He did stop me," she protested. "I really was coming to find you—"

"You needn't explain," Ethan assured her as he set the bucket down by the table. "I understand, though I doubt if my mother would. I hope you'll try to think of yourself as a lady when you're with her."

Corey felt her face flame up. "You'll have to tell me what a lady is sometime! But right now I think you might be gentleman enough to listen to me. Your mother was upset a short while ago. I quieted her, but she was asking for you—" No use to say more. Ethan had turned in a rush to go to the wagon, leaving her standing alone, feeling bruised and somehow frightened. Though it was early for supper, she began to move about the setting of the table—anything to try to outdistance the angry ring of words.

If it's going to be this way—! Forever? "Lady," he said—to sit still all day and act beautiful and read poetry, maybe? With a flicker of panic Corey knew she would never be able to do it, no matter how she might try. *Pa—you made a bad match! Why did you choose him? Hands, you said, but his hands haven't been used hard, there's no way to tell what they may be good for. And his mind's hidden so deep, to know what goes on in it would take a miracle straight out of heaven!*

When she saw Ethan step back down from the wagon, Corey glanced around feverishly, but there was no one else in sight, nowhere to retreat. And so she waited for him, poker-stiff, trying to remind herself that, for better or no, she was promised to this man. He came to a standstill before her, looking down at the broad-brimmed hat which he fiddled with, turning it around and around.

"She's asleep," he said. "When she wakens, she'll be all right again–for a while." Then with a deep breath he added, "I'm grateful for your kindness to her. I–owe you an apology."

Summoning all the dignity she could muster, Corey said, "You needn't. Only you might tell me–" Her voice got shaky and she tried again. "I'd like to know what you expected when you told Pa you'd have me."

Ethan took a grip on the hatbrim with both hands, but he met her eyes steadily. "Your father seemed to me a fine man–a gentleman. I expected his daughter to be strong and warmhearted and well raised. I wasn't disappointed; I'm not now."

"Except that it's not ladylike to split kindling?"

"I didn't mean that," he denied. "I don't want to change you, Corey. If you're more–unreserved than some young women, there's no harm in it. I can understand how a girl might have to be a bit rough-hewn to survive in this wilderness. I only spoke as I did because I hoped my mother wouldn't mistake you for a hoyden. In the world we came from everything was different; women were valued above all for their charm. But your abilities will be more useful in this trial we face —I know it and I respect you. Maybe I even envy you—" He smiled wryly. "I have no skill at chopping wood."

What is your skill, Ethan? Corey wondered silently, and as if he read the thought, he flushed. Glancing over at the other wagons, where Sister Trude and some of Millie's flock were beginning to make their appearance, he settled the hat back on his head.

"I'd best get on with my duties. The rest are about to gather for the common weal." Then curiously he asked, "Don't you occasionally feel as though you were just —say—a wheel on one of the wagons?"

In spite of the odd twist of the words, she knew what he was getting at. But the truth was that since—in all kindness—he had just called her rough-hewn, useful, and uncharming, Corey felt more like the kitchen spoon.

Six

In the days that followed Corey sensed a change in Ethan; at least to her he was a little more free-spoken. Never what you'd call talkative, but in the rare moments when they were alone he would make some remark with an oblique humor which left her feeling that he had shared something personal.

Just now, for instance, when he had brought the last pail of water over to the table where she was scouring the supper pots, he had paused beside her to watch. The others had finished the rest of the dishes and scattered off to their own groups.

"I suppose," he said, his accent crisper than usual, "that the heavens would descend in a shower of fire if someone were to take over that job from you."

"Nobody else would want it," she told him matter-of-factly.

"I'm offering my services."

Corey looked up at him past a lock of hair which had sprung loose from her sunbonnet to fall in her eyes—she couldn't shove it back because her hands were black with soot.

"I've been wanting to for quite a while," he was going on, "but I could picture the fuss it would make."

Wonderingly she said, "This is woman-work. It wouldn't be proper for you. But I'm grateful for the offer."

"I wish you wouldn't look so shocked by it," he said impatiently. "It's quite natural I should object to the sight of you, forced to scrub kettles for Shad and Meg and the rest."

Corey had thought of this herself, but she had to be honest. "Meg milks the cows for me."

"And that I don't care for, either. But since it's the order of things, at least let me help you."

She shook her head fervently. "The others wouldn't know what to make of it."

Ethan bent to scoop up a pebble, shucking it loosely in his hand, his look unfocused and discontent. "They say I hate the chores—they think I hold myself too good for manual labor. Oh, I know"—he shrugged—"I've caught their looks and remarks. They're not very subtle. Or imaginative. The true explanation wouldn't occur to them." With a swift boyish gesture he dashed the stone against the fireplace.

After he had gone, Corey went over the whole scene

again, her hands moving absently about the work. She'd always thought she had her share of imagination, but Ethan was a riddle to her, too.

It was a quiet time of evening, the last long fingers of sunlight reaching across the land. Even the campground was hushed. There weren't many people left now—all had gone west except the few families such as Tanner's who were left to aid in the final work of helping the last Saints out of Illinois. It was said that there were only a few hundred remaining now, hidden in the cellars and attics of Nauvoo—the old, the sick, the expectant mothers, and a handful of men to guard them. It was proving difficult to find homes for these disabled folk in the settlements along the Iowa side of the river. And winter would be upon them before they knew it. With just one storm out of the north, fall could set in.

". . . September's two weeks gone already and our food's near run out before we start. When do we go west, Dan?"

The rising tone of fear carried across the stillness; Corey looked over to see that several of the other men were gathered around Tanner, near the tent. As captain of the settlement he was the one they came to with their complaints. Another spoke out, his voice sharpened by anxiety.

"We ain't set up to spend a winter here, Dan. And how are we going to get across Iowa and join the others if we get snowed in?"

"Stop your bellyaching!" Tanner roared like a mad bull and they fell silent. "We'll stay here till the Council of Apostles sends for us to leave. Appears to me like you men are short on faith. Put your long faces away, go get your ladies, and be at the bowery in twenty minutes. We'll have ourselves a dance. But first, I'm going to pray over the whole back-slid lot of you!"

Corey dressed rapidly. It was the best part of this new life—the dancing. Even though Ethan never took part and she had to sit with him on the side lines, she never tired of watching. The swirl of color and stamp of feet, the drive of the music sent her blood pounding and made her feel alive in a different way than she had ever known.

She wished Ethan could share the excitement, but he hardly seemed to take any pleasure from it—just sat watching with a fixed intentness. He had said once that this sort of dancing was strange to him, but then so was it to her. If he'd only *try*— Maybe, she thought, this is where women are supposed to put stiffening in men's spirits. Looking down at herself, she surveyed the new gown with some satisfaction. Sister Elizabeth clapped her hands in outright delight.

"You're transformed, my dear! You look lovely!"

Blue velvet and black ribbons. *What will he think?* Corey walked along the narrow length of the wagon, swishing the skirt.

"Did I do that right, Miss Elizabeth?"

"Smaller steps, dear. Now come, let me put this on you." She had a little lacy cap to which she had sewed a bow of the same blue velvet. While Corey sat on the stool beside the bed, she went to work on the bronze mane of hair which was just long enough to be awkward. Corey doubted she could do much with it, but Sister Elizabeth tucked and pinned and finally sat back, almost amazed at her own results.

"Corey, child—just look at yourself!"

Self-consciously Corey took the mirror, but as she stared at the face framed there she forgot her reluctance. The freckles were fading, the hazel eyes looked dark and grave beneath the wings of soft light hair, topped by the little cap. She saw the girl in the glass begin to smile. . . .

"Thank you, ma'am," she whispered. "I don't know how—? But thank you!"

She was still smiling as she stepped out of the wagon. Ethan was waiting, pacing back and forth. When he saw her he stopped still. For a few seconds he was speechless, staring from the dress to the cap and back to her face. When he didn't speak, Corey felt her spirits falter. Quickly he covered up whatever emotion she had roused in him.

"You look quite handsome," he said uneasily. "Shall we walk along? I think Dan's waiting on us."

The bowery was a big outdoor meeting place in the center of the grove—just a roof of saplings, spliced together and thatched with brush and willows. It had been set up early last spring as a place for the campground to congregate—large enough for a hundred people or more. But tonight there weren't two dozen left to gather. The smell of autumn crispness was in the evening air, though it was still warm enough to bring out a gleam of moisture on Dan Tanner's brow as he exhorted them, standing on the platform up in front, eyes closed, long arms outstretched.

"I got these-here folks together, Lord, because they've been plagued by the Devil, lately—he's been putting doubts into their mind. But have the kindness to forgive 'em. They're worrying about what's ahead, Lord, so help 'em tighten up their bellies, because the weak-in-spirit's never going to get to Zion." He loosened his collar, and Corey knew that Dan was winding up for a long one.

"They keep fretting about food, Lord. Give 'em faith to remember that you been growing crops a long time now, and I reckon when the time comes you'll provide us with what we need."

Corey stole a glance at the hard-pressed faces of the people around. Eyes closed and heads bent, they leaned into the prayer earnestly. Most of them were poor people—cobblers, harness makers, wheelwrights—who had fled their homes without many stored-up provisions or money to buy them. Their best hope lay in the fact that the earlier parties of emigrants who had gone across Iowa last spring had planted crops at stations along the way. Later, each party of Saints to cross the state had stopped a few days in their flight to cultivate the fields, and now others were doing the reaping, but it was in everyone's mind to wonder how long this makeshift harvest would hold out.

". . . and hardship and hunger's not all we're going to have to meet!" Dan was going on powerfully. "Lord, give these children of yours the gumption to stand up against the *damnable* Missourians, too."

Corey felt a shiver go through the congregation. They all knew that before they could reach the big camp where Brigham Young had set up church headquarters they would have to pass just north of the Missouri counties where the mobs had slaughtered Mormons just ten years ago. That had especially bad memories for the Tanner family, because Sister Millie's first husband—Shad's father—had been killed at the Haun's Mill Massacre, where the mob had gunned down every Mormon in sight, even a nine-year-old boy.

"We don't want any trouble with 'em, Lord. Your book says 'forgive thine enemies' and we do. But"—Tanner's voice rose fiercely—"if they come around with guns, give us a steady hand and good aim!"

Secretly Corey glanced at Ethan, wondering what he was thinking as he stared at the floor. Could he have any idea of all that lay ahead? Whenever she thought of Sister Elizabeth and a whole wagonload of furniture and silver candlesticks and porcelain figurines, jolting along some rocky trail—

"Amen!" she joined in hastily as the prayer concluded.

"And God bless you all! Now choose up partners

for a reel. You boys get on up here." Tanner beckoned Shad and two of the other young men to take their places on the platform. One played trumpet, the others fiddles—Shad could rake off the notes like a galloping horse. While they tuned up, the women and men formed into a double line.

Corey had turned to follow Ethan over to one side, when they were brought up short by Dan himself. Heading them off, he took Corey by the arm and turned her around.

"Now here's a lass all togged out for the occasion. Daughter, I've never had the honor yet. Will you lead the set with me?"

For a moment she stood speechless. She had seen him dance with Lucy and Meg, but hadn't expected him to favor her this way.

"I'll try!" She nodded eagerly. Then added, "If it's agreeable with Brother Ethan—?"

"He'll be happy, I'm sure." Dan was leading her toward a place at the head of the line.

"I don't know the steps, sir," she confessed, with a last-minute tremor.

Tanner's black beard split wide in a white flash of teeth. "And that's what I like about you, lass—you dare a thing. Watch me, I'll lead you through." He stationed her across from him in the line of women, then clapped his hands twice and the musicians struck up sharply.

Forward they went, the two lines of dancers, and

dropped each other a bow, then back to place, and hands began to clap in rhythm. Dan beckoned Corey and she went to meet him—they hooked arms, he swung her around and sent her back. Down the line, each pair stepped out and swung in turn. Skirts swirled and the flushed faces lost some of their anxious look.

"Do-ci-do your partners!" Dan called. Corey skipped forward; she felt light as a feather. Even the velvet whirling at her ankles seemed natural and right, giving her grace. For a big man, Dan was marvelously fast—down the line they went and back, then ducked down, hand in hand, to sashay under the arch the others made. ". . . all run under!" And the dance was over.

Short of breath, glowing and laughing, she tucked up a strand of hair that had come loose. Dan dropped an arm about her shoulders with fatherly approval.

"You're quick to learn, daughter. You'll do. You'll do." As they walked across to join Ethan who stood at the far side of the bowery, Dan went on in a lower voice, "I wanted to find out if you were game, because there's somewhat we must do for the boy, yonder. For months now I been tapping around, light-like, to find out what the weakness may be, and I fear it's in the heartwood. I mislike the way he broods. The Lord made music to lighten a man's soul, and Brother Ethan is going to dance. Right now."

Hesitantly Corey dared to whisper a protest. "He's shy, sir; maybe he fears to look clumsy."

At that Dan laughed. "A dog don't learn to swim till

he's thrown in the water." As they reached Ethan, he said, with all the firmness of an axe stroke, "Here's your partner, son—and a good one she is. You'll make a fine couple in this next set."

Ethan met Tanner's look steadily. With only a slight hesitation, he said, "Yes, sir."

As he led her across to take a place in a square that was forming, Corey considered the possibility of fainting—or a sprained ankle. But when she glanced up at him, she caught a hint of distant amusement in Ethan's eyes.

Shad had stepped up to the front of the stage, his fiddle cocked against one hip—a position in which he could play as well as call the steps. Sawing off an introduction, he began to stamp his foot rhythmically.

> "Honor your partner, honor her right!
> Swing her around till the middle of the night."

And Corey was caught up and swung so hard her skirt billowed out and her feet left the floor. With as sure a step as any man there, Ethan followed the calls, guiding her into the intricacies of the spins and turns. When he met her coming around the circle in the grand-right-and-left, he whirled her into place beside him gracefully. The dance was moving too fast to puzzle over it. How it could be that he knew every call, had the whole trick of it, Corey couldn't think. All she knew was that a flood of pleasure came over her as they swung together and he lifted her in strong arms to the race of the music.

> "Fox in the chicken yard,
> Run, dog, run—"

Seven

That next morning Corey lay in bed drowsily, thinking back over the dance. With her eyes closed she could still see the pride in Ethan's look, so deep it was hidden from anyone but her. There had been secret satisfaction in his eyes as they danced. He had put one over, and it pleased him. Burying her face in the pillow, she tried to imagine that she had been part of his enjoyment, but the truth was, she knew she had little to do with it. Even though she had romped through the dance steps with a zest, thinking back over it she had an idea that compared to his poise she had seemed all elbows.

I'll practice, she vowed. *I'll learn—*

Outside, a sudden clangor broke sharply on the stillness, startling her wide awake. It was the sound of the gathering bell, not wielded with Sister Trude's rigid precision, but shaken with a feverish insistence. Scrambling out of the covers, she went across barefoot to peer out under the back flap of canvas.

In the center of the camp stood Dan, still ringing the bell with one hand while he buttoned his shirt with the other. Shad was already at work, building a fire, and now Sister Trude came hurrying, tying on an apron as she ran.

From her wagon, Millie called across, "What is it? What's happened?"

"Word's just come, we're to move on!" Dan called back. "Everybody hustle!"

When they were all seated around the big table at breakfast a half-hour later, he told them of the man who had ridden into camp at daybreak with a message from the Council.

"Brother Brigham is building a whole settlement over west of the Missouri River, trying to provide shelter for every Saint before winter sets in. Carpenters are needed. We're to go there as quick as we can. Are we ready, Sisters?"

"Near as can be." Trude nodded. "And better off than most, thanks to being thrifty with food all summer. We've got enough flour and meal to last the winter, if we're saving with it. Sister Millie and I been salting pork these past three weeks, anybody passing through that had an extra hog to trade or sell. We've got sugar and syrup enough. Only thing we're real short of is grain for the stock, and nobody's selling that these days. They won't even trade it for wool cloth or shoe leather."

Dan stroked the black beard thoughtfully. "With fifteen thousand gone ahead of us, there's not likely to be much pasture left, either."

And in a jolt it came over Corey—something she had forgotten entirely in all the muddle of her personal problems. "Pa's corn!" she whispered aloud, and they turned to look at her.

Dan prompted sharply. "Speak out, daughter!"

"There's a whole field of corn down on the bottoms if nobody's stolen it. Pa told me to offer it to you should we stay long enough. It ought to be full-dry by now, ready to shuck and shell."

"I wish you'd thought of it sooner." Tanner moved abruptly, shoving back from the table. "Trude, you and Millie stay here and pack. The young'uns and I are going to take the buckboard down and get that grain. Hop to, everybody! I want these wagons on the trail tomorrow morning, come sunup."

And a good thing it was that Judd Tremaine's clearing was far off the track. The corn stood there, untouched, yellow and bone-dry, ears hanging aslant. Piling down out of the buckboard, the children raced for it, their empty baskets knocking against their knees as they ran, while Tanner, mounted on his big bay horse, motioned Shad to drive the team over by the cabin which stood on a slight rise above the field. As the rest of them got down, Dan was already mapping the action.

"Lucy and Meg, go help pick. Shad, take the big sack and collect from their baskets, bring the corn up here quick as you get a load. Corey can shuck and Ethan and I'll shell." That was the meanest part, of course—it took tough hands to strip the hardened grain off the ears.

Shucking was a job which Corey would hardly have preferred but she settled herself on the doorstep of the cabin. Shad was already coming back with a small load of ears which he dumped at her feet with a wink.

"Now we'll see if a fellow can learn to shell corn as quick as he took to dancing." He glanced at Ethan, who was helping Dan get the big grain sacks out of the wagon.

Down in the field a chatter was rising as the children spread out along the rows—Corey saw Sammy hit Staley with an ear of corn, heard Meg chide them sharply. Then Dan shouted down.

"That's enough jabber! Work gets done faster quiet."

After that, a buzzing stillness settled over the clearing, broken only by the dry clash of stalks, the fall of corn into the baskets. Working swiftly, Corey peeled the ears bare and pitched them onto a pile between the two men, who sat on the tailgate of the wagon with the sacks open before them.

Though Ethan's grip was strong, his hands were no match for Tanner's calloused fingers. Dan could clean an ear with one twist and pick up the next so fast that the grain seemed to spurt from his fingers in a steady golden stream.

"Take hold harder, boy," he muttered once. "Blisters won't hurt you—just build tougher skin, which you'll be needing."

After that there was no more talk. The homesickness that had been trying to pluck at Corey got a good clutch on her, and she had to fight off a whole flock of memories. The way she and Pa had planted this field last spring, laughing and talking about how they would harvest it and sell the grain, then go west together, on horseback, traveling light. It seemed a long, long time ago. No telling where he might be by now. The papers said the Mormon Battalion was halfway to Sante Fe, wherever that was—somewhere in Mexico. Marching. Pa always did hate to go afoot.

"What was that?" Tanner straightened and held still, listening. "Did you hear—?"

And then it came again from far away—the sharp report of shots. Scattered at first, then volley after volley, punctuated by a deeper roar.

"That sounded like cannon!" Dan was on his feet. The younger ones down in the field had paused to listen, too. Down the wind came another crackle of gunfire—they could hear now that it was coming from across the river. Again the dull thunder of the big gun.

In a hushed voice Corey said, "the mob must be getting terrible bold, to raid in daylight."

"That's no shivaree, not with fieldpieces," Dan said grimly. "Sounds like the wolves are moving in for the finish." Motioning impatiently to the workers, he called, "Double-fast! I want that field picked clean as a chickenbone." To Corey and Ethan he added, "You two get on down there and help. I'll shell as much as there's time for. The rest can be done later. I want to get up to the ferry landing. They're going to be coming across in a scramble, and they'll be needing help—what's left of 'em."

The river road to the boat dock followed the top of the Iowa bluffs. Bumping along in the wagon, Corey could look down upon the whole terrible scene spread out in painful detail below. Boats tossed and struggled in the roily water—skiffs, log rafts, anything that could be rowed. Even children could be seen hauling on the oars. Some of the craft were being swept downstream on the current; others clustered around the heavy-laden ferries, so packed with people and stock, the water lapped the decks. On the far side of the river more people could be seen running down the hill away from the city, while cannon fire still rumbled behind them. Around the landing over there a huddle of humanity bunched.

"I don't understand!" Corey stared down at the scene with shock and dismay. She was seated on the driver's box of the wagon beside Ethan, who had been chosen to drive the team while Dan and Shad had galloped ahead on the bay horse. "Those poor folk are harmless," she went on, aghast. "Old and sick. Why should anyone want to hurt them?"

"It's a wretched quirk of human nature, I grant you." Ethan sounded grim. He was driving as fast as the rutted road would permit, handling the horses with remarkable skill.

"How could you call it 'human'?" Corey demanded.

"Because it is. Very."

"Well, perhaps—in your country—"

"This is my country now," he told her tensely. "That's why I've given it a good deal of thought. Do you really not understand what is happening over there? It's the hysteria of victory by a scrawny lot of ruffians over a powerful community which once threatened them. Oh, yes, they felt threatened. The Mormons were bringing order to their frontier—Mormon law. And growing in numbers with every day. On the boat that brought us across from England were five hundred other converts. All of a single purpose and faith. And obedience. Did you know that the Church elected the last governor of Illinois? I can well imagine how such absolute discipline could terrify a lonely backwoods farmer who feels himself and his few neighbors in a minority. It's not difficult to understand—nor does that excuse what they're doing."

Corey listened, puzzled. He spoke with such detachment—and yet he was obviously almost as distressed by the scene below as she was. He was putting the wagon over the road at a wrenching pace.

"Hold on tight, please," he called over his shoulder to the others who sat behind in the wagon bed, clinging to the sides. "We're going down a rough stretch." Reins in one hand and the other on the brake, he brought them down the tight descent from the rim of the bluff to the river shore, hardly slackening pace. When they rolled out across the bottoms toward the ferry landing, Corey let out her breath in a shaky sigh.

But even after watching it all from the heights, she was hardly prepared for the scene around the dock. The feeble and wounded lay on thin pallets or bare earth; the older folk were dull-eyed with suffering. Some of the younger men—all that was left of the Temple Guard—were trying to bind up their own wounds with rags. Those able to stand milled helplessly, too numb with shock to assist the others. Livestock roamed untended—and a sorry-looking lot it was. In their final desperation the refugees had herded together every old swaybacked horse or dry milch cow that could be found.

Two ferries were unloading at the dock—Dan and Shad were busy carrying the infirm and wounded ashore. Corey and the others piled out of the wagon and hurried to the landing, to help, but by the time they got there, the big barges were nearly empty. With a start of recognition Corey saw her Elder, leading two frightened children off the boat. He was dirty and disheveled, his face streaked with blood where a musket ball had grazed it. As he came over to the Tanners, he seemed not to see or know Corey. He looked unutterably weary.

To Dan he said hoarsely, "Bless you, Brother, your help here is appreciated, but we can manage to get these people disembarked. What they need most is clothing—bedding—pots and pans. Wagons and teams—whatever you have, in the name of God it must be shared. If you have valuables, they can be bartered for food at the settlements up the river. I'm afraid these poor homeless will have to abide here for some time. They can't be moved any farther for a while."

Dan said, "We've had our orders to head on west, Elder, but if you say the word we'll stay and help care for them."

The Elder shook his head. "Do as the Council has instructed. Go on ahead and help prepare a place for the rest of us when we can make the trip. I'd say to travel as rapidly as possible. Bear the word to those at the advance stations to strip themselves of every scrap they can spare. Don't let them refuse you. Above all, food—!"

Dan nodded. Beckoning the family, he led the way back to the buckboard. Climbing in, he threw down two heavy sacks of shelled corn. "Shad, Ethan, take those to the Elder. Ethan—?" He looked around angrily.

To one side, the boy was down on his knees beside a wounded man who lay on the ground. He seemed to be trying to dress a bleeding bullet hole, but even in that he was hardly adept, tying a strip of cloth around the arm above the wound, twisting it senselessly tight. Corey swallowed with chagrin; Dan's face went dark but he shut his jaws, for the Elder had come up to take the other sack of grain.

"This will help," he said, hefting it to his shoulder.

"At least it may quiet the stock." Dan glanced at the scrawny animals.

"Brother"–the Elder spoke with an abiding dignity –"this will feed human bellies tonight, what ones of them can down it. For the rest, all we can do is pray."

Eight

"What about a pair of silver candlesticks?" Sister Trude asked flatly, confronting Dan in the early light of that next morning. "They'd bring a-plenty up in the settlements. Some folks would give a whole beef steer for fancy doodads like them."

Tanner hesitated. Not once in that long, hectic night had he held back on anything. The buckboard and team he had donated first, plus a milch cow and a bullock, then supervised the dividing of everything else they had, from hams to harness strap. The other Sugar Creek families had brought what little they could spare, but it was understood that they were thinly supplied themselves, and Dan accepted the burden of heavy giving. Utensils, clothes, bedding—once Sister Millie had gone off crying when he had demanded four of her best quilts, but she had soon come back and apologized.

Through it all Sister Trude had been firm as granite. And just about as gray, too, when she saw the food being stowed in the buckboard. Now, there was challenge in her voice—the first time Corey had seen one of the womenfolk talk up to Dan.

Slowly he said, "In the beginning Sister Elizabeth gave the most—money, flat silver, all her jewelry—"

"We gave ours, too, even if it wasn't so much." Sister Trude didn't yield an inch.

At last Dan nodded. "Hitch up, Shad. I'll be back in a minute." And yet when he returned from his third wife's wagon, carrying the candle sconces, he was troubled, as if it grieved him personally to part with them.

Corey glanced sidelong at Ethan, but he hardly seemed aware of what was going on. All through the packing and preparation he had been preoccupied and restless.

When Shad had finished harnessing the team, Dan said, "Go on, then, drive these things over to the landing as quick as you can. Take my horse along and get back with all speed. Meanwhile, I'll be getting our wagons on the trail. You'll likely catch us before we're well out of camp. The rest of you—"

"Sir." Ethan spoke quietly but it startled them all. "Let me deliver these things. Shad will be of more use to you here than I could." There was suppressed urgency in the appeal.

Dan eyed him uncertainly. "I doubt you could handle my horse on the way back."

"If that worries you, I'll take Corey's mare." Ethan insisted with a deference that was almost painful, it was so laced with intensity.

Dan was perplexed, but plainly tempted. "Well, if you'll make the trip quickly—we need every hand here to get us along the road as fast as we can move."

Ethan was already on his way to his mother's wagon, with some scattered explanation that he must tell her he was going.

"If he steps out like that, I'll be satisfied," Dan said curiously. "Odd, though. It's the first time the boy's ever offered to do a thing, much less begged for it."

Corey had her own misgivings as she bridled Peggy. It had occurred to her that she was going to have to care for Sister Elizabeth through this difficult moment of uprooting, and a qualm of anxiety came over her at the prospect. When she brought the mare to the buckboard Ethan was waiting. As he tied Peggy beside the cow and bullock, he was speaking in a low tone.

"Mother seemed to be getting confused and distraught. I believe I've calmed her—she's gone back to sleep. I doubt you'll have any trouble, but if she wakens and seems nervous, don't give her tea—just warm some milk if you can. It will soothe her." He swung up onto the driver's seat, then paused to look down at Corey a moment, disturbed. "I'm sorry to leave you just at this time, but there's something I must do." With a slap of the reins, he started the horses off at a brisk pace toward the river.

There was no time to wonder what he meant. Dan was calling to know whose wagon was ready to take the trail. Corey thought she was as ready as she'd ever be. She and Ethan had worked most of the night, packing the delicate gewgaws and tying the furniture in place. Since their load was heavy, they hadn't been assigned any bags of grain or provisions. Most of the food was packed solid in the bed of the big freight wagon, where the three men would sleep on feather mattresses thrown across the top of the sacks and boxes. Sister Trude was taking the cookery utensils in her wagon, and Millie had the loom and spinning wheel to make place for among the jumble of youngsters. It was a tired lot who gathered around Dan, but they were all able to say they were ready to yoke up.

"Let's get to it, then!" He gave them their orders: The women were to turn the stock out and start them down the trail—milch cows, horses, the young bulls that had been brought along for beef. Meg and Corey were assigned to keep the youngsters out of harm's way—they were jumping with excitement, squealing and pummeling each other. It was all the two girls could do to keep them from getting under the massive feet of the oxen as Dan and Shad led the big animals, yoked in pairs, lumbering through the camp and up to the wagons.

Once as they came past, hauling at a pair of snorting bullocks, rebellious under the yoke, Corey chanced to catch Meg watching Shad. For all the girl usually gave him the sharp edge of her tongue, in that instant a secret softness showed in her look. When she realized that Corey had glimpsed it, she flushed.

"Good thing," she remarked pertly, "that Ethan chose the easy job. Takes a strong man to handle those critters when they've not been used for months."

Corey couldn't help teasing a little. "Shall I mention to Brother Shad how you admire his muscle?"

"He's no brother of mine!" Meg denied swiftly. "Only by marriage." And it came over Corey that, tartness or no, Meg really was in love.

The sun was only nine-o'clock high when the last team was in place—three yokes to haul Dan's big wagon, two each for Sister Trude's and Millie's. Sister Elizabeth's wagon required three pair to draw it. Corey stood surveying the six mighty creatures, their skins sleek and tight from rich feeding all summer, their big heads restive under the heavy collar of wood.

"Can you handle 'em, daughter?" Dan had come up beside her.

Corey thought he'd not have asked if he hadn't believed she could. "I reckon, sir, if you'll show me how."

"You've got a whip and a goad. But mostly it's done with the voice. Speak 'em firm. Listen to the way I do, and sound as if you mean it. I'll put you third in line, so's you can't fall behind. Steady does it. How's Elizabeth taking this?"

"Well enough, sir. She's resting in bed."

"Good. Then we'll go." Striding back across the camp, he took his place by the lead wagon. Shad had gone ahead with the herd, which would have to be driven before them all the way. Trude and Millie were ready beside their teams. With one last look around, Dan took up his whip, cracked it in the air sharp as a pistol shot.

"*Ai-yaaah!*" he shouted, and the big wagon moved out.

Sister Trude followed, wielding the goad with a firm hand, and Millie motioned to Corey to go next. Looking at her stamping team, she fingered the whip, took a deep breath, and whacked the ground.

"Move!"

They stood, blinking and surly.

Taking firmer hold, Corey brought the whip down across their backs. "*Gid-aaaap!*"

Grudgingly, the big beasts threw their weight into the yoke, the wagon creaked and groaned and began to roll. They were on their way west.

In the breathless heat of that Indian summer afternoon everything mingled into one vast torment—the dust, the screech of wheels, the beat of the sun straight down, and the ache of a body that had only a scant hour or two of sleep. Corey trudged along doggedly, goading the oxen, no longer shy of them. She didn't even hesitate to take them by the nose ring and lead them around the boulders and pits in the trail.

The train moved so slowly she could hardly judge how far they had come, but the question beginning to pound in her mind was of Ethan. A dozen pictures kept rising to worry her—a horse gone lame, maybe a fall, or a brush with some Missourian. She was thankful when she saw Lucy drop back along the trail to join her. She had come to be able to talk to Lucy freely.

"How are you making out?" the older girl asked as she came up.

"Well enough. But I keep wondering where Ethan could be."

"He'll be along." Lucy laughed reassuringly. "He may be slow, but he never gives up. You should have seen his do-or-die patience when he was learning to dance."

"Learning? How? Who—?"

"I showed him how to swing and turn—just the knack of it. He'd already memorized the steps from watching the others. But I'll tell you a secret: To Ethan, anything less than perfect is unworthy. My, you never saw anyone worry over a thing so!"

"But why?" Corey stared at her blankly. "Why should he go to all that bother?"

"I haven't the least idea." Lucy's long, homely face quirked with mockery.

"For me?" Corey queried faintly.

"He said, every time there was a dance you were wishful as a child in a candy store. Of course I'm betraying him—he never expected me to give him away, but I thought you ought to know. He's such a strange one, so different from the rest of us and so awfully conscious of it."

"That must be why he wanted to get away this morning, to keep from bungling something when we broke camp," Corey mused. "But it doesn't explain why he hasn't caught up with us yet."

"From what little I know of him, I'd say Ethan is probably thinking of something else." Lucy laughed ruefully. "It's too bad, because Papa is going to be asking questions, too." She was watching Dan come back along the trail, riding his big bay. "I think I'd better go help Mama with the team. Poor brutes, they're taking a real drubbing today."

She trudged on forward as Tanner wheeled his horse and swung down. He fell into step beside Corey, fanning himself with his hat, his dark brows knit with displeasure.

"Where is he? What in tarnation is keeping him?"

"Maybe the mare went lame," Corey suggested.

"He could have been here by now, even riding at a stumble-foot walk!" Dan took the whip from her and cracked it over the oxen—they stepped out with new respect. "Daughter, I'm sorry you've been worked so hard. The others have been getting some rest. You climb up and ride a spell, I'll drive your teams."

"No, sir, thank you. I don't mind."

"How's Sister Elizabeth?" he asked.

"Still sleeping."

Tanner fixed her with those gleaming black eyes, full of disbelief, then dawning comprehension and anger. "By thunder, if that young whelp has given her some devil's brew again to make her sleep—!" Handing her the whip and the reins of his horse, he went back to climb in at the rear of the wagon. He was only gone a minute. When he returned his face was livid with anger. "As soon as he comes, send him forward to see me at once," he told her curtly. Swinging up into the saddle, he cantered toward the front of the train.

But by the time they made their encampment late that afternoon, Ethan still hadn't caught up with them.

"Is your mare slow-paced?" Sister Trude asked Corey as they all pitched into the preparation of supper.

"No, ma'am," she had to admit. "Peggy's stout—she can go along at a lope for hours."

No more was said. The women got a stew boiling and bread set to bake in the oven which Shad dug for them.

"What with the heat and the jolting," Lucy admitted, "I doubt if the dough rose properly. Bread probably won't be any good."

But it was. The best, Corey thought, she had ever eaten. Silently, hungrily, they dug in, each seated on whatever log or rock came handiest, too wearied to makeshift a table. Even the children were droopy-eyed and hushed as they ate.

After the meal, Shad went to round up the stock while Dan sawed lengths from the timber he had felled for tomorrow's firewood. Each person went to his work without question—Sister Trude's training had taken effect. Only Corey delayed her own chores to take a bowl of broth in to Sister Elizabeth.

She roused sleepily, long enough to eat and smile

her thanks, before drifting off again. Corey had been thinking of what Dan said—it began to make sense that Ethan must have given his mother some draught to quiet her, but it was a shocking thought! Potions were not permitted by those of the faith. As Pa had often told her, doctors and medicine men were quacks—fakers. "The Bible sets forth all you need to know of healing," he would say. "The Lord gives us suffering for some reason—only faith can make you well again." And of course she, herself, had read about Job. And Lazarus. But then Sister Elizabeth's trouble was just slightly different, she thought.

Troubled, she covered the slumbering woman with an extra quilt to guard against the coming chill of evening, then took the bowl back out to the fireplace. There she found Sister Trude finishing the pots and kettles while Millie started tomorrow's bread—another of Corey's duties. When they saw the look of dumfounded gratitude on her face, the two women smiled.

"You've done your share today," Millie said.

Trude added, "And someone else's, too—" But she broke off short as they heard a sound—hoofbeats coming along the back trail at a gallop.

Dan put down his axe and strode over to the center of the clearing, fists anchored to his hips, black beard bristling. Shad had finished making a rope enclosure to hold the animals for the night. Moving heavily, he went over to the wash bucket and began to douse his face with cold water. The others stood, watchful, as

Ethan rode in. Dusty and sweated, he slid down off the mare's back and walked over slowly to face them.

"Saul"—Dan beckoned Millie's ten-year-old—"take the horse, walk her and water her, and stake her out where she can get grass. The rest of you young'uns get to bed. Quick."

They scattered without a murmur, for Dan's voice had an ominous ring. "Now," he went on to Ethan, who stood stiffly, waiting, "I want to know what kept you."

In a voice so strained they could hardly hear him he said, "I stayed and helped a while at the landing."

"Who asked you to? The Elder?"

"No, sir. No one. I just thought I should."

"Do you remember, I told you to come straight after us? Did you disobey me of a purpose?"

"I didn't think of it that way."

"You thought—you didn't think!" Dan said grimly. "Did it enter your mind that there was others here, put to hardship by you? In these times, thinking is a job for one man, if this family is to push through to headquarters before snow. We're under orders—I'm under 'em, you're under 'em. You feel you're specially favored, to decide when you will and won't obey?"

Ethan shook his head. His look was fixed on the ground at his feet. At his sides, his hands were clenched.

"I've been trying to bring you along easy, boy," Dan went on sternly, "but I begin to see it's not the way, so we'll try it different. From now on you'll do your share and more—if you work slow, you'll have to put in extra hours. You'll fetch water night and morning, yoke your own wagon and drive it. You'll fell trees and you'll dig and you'll smith and mend harness, and when the rest of us need a hand, you'd better be there before you're asked. What's more, if you can't get to supper table on time, you'll go hungry. Do you understand? Don't nod—I want an answer!"

"I understand." Ethan was white as paper, but the words came distinctly.

"Then you can begin on that pile of logs—they're to be split and stacked, ready for breakfast tomorrow morning. What we don't use then, we'll carry along for noon meal. You can get to work."

"May I go and see how my mother is first?" Ethan asked in a low voice.

"We'll both go," Tanner said.

Corey slipped on ahead of them and got the lamp lit in the wagon. Sister Elizabeth was breathing gently, evenly—she didn't stir as the two men came in. For a moment they stood, looking down at her silently, while Corey stayed quiet in the shadows.

"You gave her some kind of infernal drug, didn't you?" Dan muttered at last in a throaty whisper.

Ethan didn't answer at once. He reached out to take his mother's hand lightly, pressing his fingers against her wrist. "She's come through this first hard day well. Isn't that the important thing?"

"Not if she's hexed. Where's the stuff? I want it."

Ethan hesitated.

"Listen to me!" Dan thrust the younger man around to face him. "I'll not have anyone in my family who leagues with the Devil. I'll turn you out first!"

Ethan reached over to open a drawer in the bedside table, took out a small vial of liquid, and handed it to Dan. Tanner shoved it in his pocket.

"Now I will tell you one thing: If you ever again, for any reason, steal off to the den of some apothecary for more of this, I'll be forced to try and drive the evil spirit out of you in a way you won't like. I advise you try some prayers of your own first."

As they turned to go, they saw Corey, and both men looked startled.

"Could I make you some tea?" she asked of Ethan.

Dan answered. "No, daughter, get to bed." Shoving the boy ahead of him, he went out into the darkness.

Bone-tired as she was, Corey huddled under the covers, wide awake and pulsing with confused emotions. Fear and some premonition of trouble; puzzlement over Ethan. But along with it was an unreasoning sympathy that brought a twinge inside her every time she heard the fall of the axe, coming so slowly and unevenly from the other side of the camp. It went on for a long time—far into the depths of the night.

Nine

"Marlowe has a fearful line in one of his plays, about hell being right here on earth." Sister Elizabeth shrank back against the pillows and stared up anxiously at the single small lantern which hung above her bed—it was swinging wildly as the wagon swayed. Corey was trying to sew by the unsteady light, but it was mostly pretense. When she did poke the needle in, it usually came home in her finger.

Besides, she was hungry. They were all on short rations, now—each way station they reached had already sent back every bit of food that could be spared to the Poor Camp on the river. After the Tanners had left Locust Creek without being able to replenish their supplies by so much as a box of tea, Sister Trude had got out her sheets of paper and begun to divide people into loaves of bread and portions of meat. The result was that each member of the company was limited to just so much, according to the amount of work he did. And Corey's share was not especially generous, since she spent most of her days riding with Sister Elizabeth.

Today, what with the heavy rain coming down, there'd been no hot meal at noon—just a bit of cheese, an apple, and two slices of bread for each of the women. Corey had broken up Sister Elizabeth's bread into some milk and had spread her own with lard, of which they had a good supply. But by midafternoon she was beginning to feel dreary inside.

"Oh, dear, I can't remember that passage. I wish I could look it up, but it's too dark." Sister Elizabeth kept watching the lantern, which was throwing shadows in crazy patterns. "Why must we go on and on like this? California can't be so far—nothing could be this far. We must be going in circles!"

Quickly Corey went to her side, plumped the pillows, and straightened the shawl around her shoulders. "No, it's a long way off yet. Brother Dan says we must keep going. It's all right." That usually had a good effect—Sister Elizabeth always seemed uplifted by Dan's prayers, which he said over her regularly each morning. Now she looked at Corey distractedly.

"Who—? Who did you say?"

"Ethan says so, too. Now try to rest." Corey edged past the bedstead and loosened the front canvas enough to look out. "Ethan—" she called softly.

Through the curtain of rain she saw the gray figure up ahead turn, then wave to show he had heard and understood. Leaving the oxen, he sloshed forward through the mud, lost to sight in the downpour. Before he could halt the wagon for any reason he had to ask permission of Dan, though Tanner never refused when it was for Sister Elizabeth's sake.

These two weeks had been hard on Ethan. The pressure had been unrelenting. Ordered to do all the work at which he was so awkward, he had struggled silently to achieve by endurance what he couldn't with skill. Yet try as he might, he couldn't bring himself to yell properly at the oxen; they tended to lag until Dan finally stationed him second in line. Plodding along, day after day, behind Dan's big freight van, Ethan had eaten dust and criticism with equal patience, though there were times when Corey thought she glimpsed a sort of desperation deep in his eyes.

It made her stretch out toward the boy, secretly; she wished that she might help him. Now as he came back along the trail she called quietly, "Let me drive them a while."

He shook his head. "We're going to make camp here for the night. Tell Mother I'll be in shortly."

Going back to the bedside, Corey put an arm around Sister Elizabeth to steady her as the wagon began to wheel into a circle with the others. "We're stopping now. When Ethan comes he'll help you remember that poem."

She breathed easier when the lurching old box came to a halt. Hurrying to light the candles in the tiny stove, she set a pot of tea on to boil. When, in a minute, she heard Ethan outside scraping the mud off his boots, hanging up his coat, Corey hastily tucked the stray tendrils of hair up under the ribbon of her cap and straightened her apron, warm with an anticipation that flustered her.

He came in, ducking under the canvas and stepping over the tailgate stiffly, as if his limbs ached. She saw that his clothes were drenched; the rain had soaked right through his coat and his dark hair was plastered wetly across his forehead. Yet he said, "Good evening" to them as if he'd just come from a pleasant stroll.

As he went over to his mother's bed, the hard-pressed set of his face eased. With a smile that made him seem years younger, he took her hands and kissed them lightly in one of those little gestures of respect that he could bring off so well. As he sat down, Corey brought him a cup of tea. With one quick look he thanked her.

". . . and I've been trying this last hour to remember a line from Faustus–I think it was Faustus–" Sister Elizabeth was saying. "Something about man's trials on earth."

Ethan sipped the steaming drink. "Let me see. Was it this one: 'Act well your part–there, all the honor lies'?"

"No, no! That's Pope." She sat up straighter, a faint

freshness coming back to the waxen cheeks. "The one I mean—"

Corey left them. She had come to realize that they liked to be alone, at least a small part of the time. They created a sort of world around themselves that was far away from a dripping camp in the Iowa forest. She was glad for them, but it left her feeling more alone than ever.

It was a hasty supper they got together that late afternoon; wood too wet to burn and children too hungry to wait. The potatoes were a little raw and the meat flavored with smoke, but the warmth of the stew helped drive off the chill.

After dishes had been cleared away, Sister Millie reminded them that one of her wagon wheels was sticking worse and worse, now that the weather had turned damp.

Dan sighed and summoned Shad to come help him raise the heavy vehicle on blocks. To Ethan he said, "You'll have to round up the stock alone. Don't be too long about it, either—darkness'll come early tonight."

The animals seldom wandered far, tired as they were after a day on the trail, but they could be obstinate about herding together, so there was really no reason for the growing misgiving Corey felt, as a half-hour passed and Ethan didn't return. Dan and Shad, absorbed in their repair work, seemed not to have noticed. It occurred to her that she might as well slip off and help him without their ever knowing.

Putting on a heavy cloak and hood, she stole off into the woods. The sky was low, the scud of clouds just brushing the treetops, but for the moment the rain had let up and she could follow Ethan's trail easily across a muddy little stream and down to a meadow. The cattle were there; they must have scented pasture and gone to it. On the far side of the field she saw a shadowy figure, poking around the bushes.

"Ethan?" she called softly.

He stepped out into the clearing and she went to him.

"Did Dan send you?" He sounded irritable.

"No. I came because I thought you might need help."

With an exasperated gesture, he said, "Mehitable's missing. I've been looking for her this half-hour."

Corey glanced at the herd and saw that the big white cow was not among them.

"It's as if these animals are possessed," he went on with a touch of desperation. "They never misbehave or stray except when I'm herding. Do they know that I'm a dunce at this? Are they that perceptive?"

Quickly she said, "That cow's just naturally cantankerous. I'll go look for her while you take the others to camp."

"No!" he protested. "I can't do that—leave you out here in the woods alone."

"You must!" she urged him. "Dan'll be expecting you to bring the cattle in by dark. Please, Ethan, it will mean another scene. Besides, I can take care of myself."

He laughed, and there was the sound of discouragement in it. "What you mean is, I'd be more hindrance than help." Turning away, he began to drive the herd ahead of him up the meadow, chucking clods of wet earth at them with a disheartened gesture in which there was a whole world of defeat.

Brimming with remorse, but with no time to grieve over it, Corey began to skirt the lower edge of the clearing, in search of some sort of path. It seemed unlikely to her that even a tough-skinned old creature like Mehitable would have chosen to leave the meadow for the thick bushes where Ethan had been looking. Coming across a narrow track through the woods, she followed it. There were hoofprints a-plenty, as though many animals used it, horses as well as cattle. It made her uneasy, for it must mean a farm nearby. Quietly she moved along, listening for any sound that might lead her to the cow, but the woods were silent on every side. And then, suddenly, they gave way—she found herself on the verge of a clearing.

A cabin, a shed, and a fenced-in dooryard where a dozen pigs rooted around the edge of a muddy little pond—Corey took in the scene swiftly, including Mehitable who stood tied to a tree not far from the cabin. From inside the building came the sound of men's voices, laughing, talking along in a nasal twang. It was a little like Pa's manner of speech, and he'd grown up in the Ozarks. Corey thought, uneasily, that these were likely Missourians!

Shivering, she stood undecided, then a daring impulse won over and she moved softly out across the clearing toward the captive cow. She had just reached her side when Mehitable let out a long bellow of welcome. There was a clatter from the cabin and two men burst from the door, carrying lanterns.

"Hah!" the younger of them yelled excitedly, "it's a girl come to claim the critter."

The older man held up his lamp—Corey saw a heavy face stubbled with unkempt whiskers.

"Does she look like a Mormon, Pap?" the boy demanded.

"What else? Nobody but them's going across here with stock this time of year." They looked her over curiously. "It's just like 'em, to send their women out at night to do man's work. They think not that of a girl." He snapped his fingers. "Keep 'em by the dozen, just like so many cattle. Time them Elders get through working 'em they ain't worth as much as a good cow."

Corey reached out and jerked the rope free of the tree. "If you'll stand aside, I'll just take *our* cow back to where she belongs—unless maybe you brought her here a-purpose and aim to keep her, like a thief?"

"She talks big," commented the boy.

"Yeh. Especially since them prophets and apostles is the biggest thieves ever born. Take all the land in sight, set up their cities, and their talk about how nobody else got any rights on this green earth, or heaven, either. Next thing you know, whang-o, they've took over a whole county just like you'd pick an apple. Would've took over the state, too, if we hadn't run 'em out."

Corey was edging away when the older man reached out and caught her by the shoulder. "You just stand still whiles I figger out what to do with you."

"If we turn her loose, she'll likely bring the whole lot of 'em down here, we'll lose the cow, too," the boy said. "Let's keep her."

"That'll bring 'em, too. They don't like to lose this kind of property, neither." The man eyed her with a slight smile and Corey felt a stir of fear. In a surge of fury, she struck at the ragged face with her doubled fist and almost broke free.

"Why, you little vixen!" He handed his lantern to the boy, then caught her roughly, twisting her wrists behind her and holding them clamped in one of his hands while with the other he shoved back the hood. The light hair fell about her shoulders—as he viewed it, the smile broadened. "Maybe we will keep her at that. We could use a girl to scrub up the place."

"Lemme have her, Pap," the boy pleaded. "You said I could take a wife."

"Wife! Mormons you don't marry—"

Corey kicked him as hard as she could. The man gasped and his smile vanished. "That ain't polite. You know what we do to folks that ain't polite? We baptize 'em, so's they get to be good little saints again." Picking her up in spite of her struggles, he carried her toward the pig pond. They were at the fence—Corey could smell the stench of the mudhole—when a voice cut in.

"Put the young lady down—gently."

The two men whirled and Corey saw Ethan, mounted on Peggy. He was looking down the gleaming twin cylinders of a double-barreled pistol.

The Missouri boy murmured uneasily, "He don't sound like a Mormon."

A shot roared in the stillness of the clearing, the ball skimmed the older man's hat from his head. With an oath, he dropped Corey—she scrambled to one side, leaving the two men standing isolated in the lamplight.

"Next time I'll aim lower," Ethan told them. "Cross over the fence."

"Now, by jingo—!"

"Quickly. I have another pistol here with lead enough for both of you." As they climbed into the pigpen he added, "Go on, into the mud." Glumly they waded a few steps into the pond, sinking into the odorous muck up to their knees.

By now Corey had started the cow along the trail. Wheeling the mare, Ethan leaned down and scooped her up to ride in front of him. Over his shoulder he told the men, "If you really hunger for trouble, come looking. We'll accommodate you." Then digging heels into the horse, he set a good pace up the dark trail, Mehitable bobbing ahead of them, a white blob in the night.

When they reached the meadow again, Ethan slowed the mare to a walk while he shoved the pistol into his belt beneath his shirt. "It was fortunate they didn't rush me," he remarked in his constrained British way. "That second gun was a bit of bluff."

Corey was trembling with reaction. She had a terrible desire to laugh or cry, or both. She could still hear the sing of the bullet. "Did you really mean to take off his hat?" she quavered weakly.

"I'm sorry that startled you, but I thought I'd better do it. I didn't want them to rally their wits—they might have started into the cabin with you. I'm not sure I could have brought myself to shoot one of them. You may as well know that—as a bad man, I'm a fraud." His arm tightened around her shoulders. "I'm a fool, too. I should never have let you talk me into leaving you."

Corey clung to him. "I almost made a ruination of things, boasting about being able to take care of myself." And a whole tide of confession was at her lips, ready to burst out. She wanted to tell him that she was ashamed and grateful, and that his arm around her was giving her a warm comfort such as she'd never known before. But Ethan was going on, a little wearily:

"Don't blame yourself, Corey. And don't lose that confidence! You're quick and sure—I've wanted to tell you this a hundred times, but haven't been able to find the words so you'll understand and not take it amiss."

"Tell me what?"

"That I know you're too strong to be bound to a man like me who is neither confident nor capable. I don't intend to marry you—I never have. No, don't ask me questions, I don't feel that I could possibly answer them truthfully. I've become a frightful liar in these past months. I just hope you can find someone worthy of you—in all these thousands there must be a man you can care for. I promise to help you get our vows lifted when the time comes. I'd never wed a girl who hadn't chosen me—likely not even one who had."

Corey was left speechless. Stammering for words, she said, "But it will . . . change everything . . ."

"Not for the present. You need the outward guise to keep your place with the others. This is just a matter between you and myself, but perhaps it will give you some peace of mind." He spoke with a grave finality that was beyond doubt. Then, as he saw the lights of camp ahead, he added with a touch of bitterness, "Dan thinks I'm of no special worth. When it comes to my real futility, there are all shades and degrees that he doesn't begin to know."

PART TWO

Ten

"This'll be some different," Sister Trude warned. "You reckon you can handle it?"

Corey nodded quickly. "I kept house for Pa and me."

"You'll find this some harder. If you're going to cook meals for Sister Elizabeth and Ethan, separate from the common table, you'll have to learn to stretch food. This-here's all we've got for the whole winter." She motioned around the small cellar where they stood. It was full of barrels of flour and sacks of meal and potatoes, baskets of apples, crocks of lard, and the like. But Corey was secretly alarmed to think how many people would have to live off these supplies—and for how long.

"I reckon you'll slaughter a beef now and then," she ventured.

"That'll be up to the Council. When we get to Zion,

we'll need herds, so don't count on much meat this winter. Just make do with these stores—this is your share right here along this wall. I'll keep watch to see how you come along, but I'll leave it to you to manage. It'll be good training. That's why I agreed to the notion."

When they had reached Winter Quarters on the Missouri it had been Dan's idea to build a separate house for each of his wives. And because Sister Elizabeth was kept to her bed, he was willing to let Corey fix their meals apart.

"Divide your goods into months—so much for December and don't steal from January," Sister Trude was going on in her flat, fussy way. "Don't cook foolish. Never fry. Boil. Drink off the broth, too, so you get all the strength out of everything. Be sure to sprout your potatoes regular and don't run short of onions. If a man gets the nervous indigestion, there's nothing for it like onions. I'd say that fellow of yours is going to need a-plenty."

"Yes'm!" Corey agreed, so fervently it made the older woman smile.

"Don't worry, child. All men turn fretful sometimes. Ethan's not so feckless as Dan thinks—leastways I've got my private notion about that. But the boy's far off. You'll have to be the one tends to details."

"He's so far away I can't reach him," Corey confessed.

"Don't pester. The more you listen, the more he'll

talk. Mainly all a girl can do is keep the household running so he won't snag over little things. Keep track of the money or food or whatever you've got, but do it private. Men don't like to know they're being managed. And don't scold—at least not much. Decide for yourself what's important and don't mention what's not. Mainly feed him as well as you can. Put plenty of salt in thin soup." Then as she turned away, her face hidden by the shadows, she added, "Some folks say a man runs on his heart. I say it's his belly." And with that she began to climb the steps out of the cellar. Sidling between the barrels and sacks, Corey followed her out into the gray daylight. Together they let down the door that closed the entrance to the dugout.

"That's going to get heavy, with snow on it," Trude observed. A few flakes were falling now out of the cottony thick sky, and the river below had a sullen winter tarnish. Along its banks, from neat rows of tents and huts, smoke rose in hundreds of thin blue streamers. The settlement clustered thick all over the bottoms on both sides of the river.

Corey's look went instinctively to the big log structure going up at the water's edge not far away—a gristmill it was to be, to grind wheat that had been reaped in haste, back in Illinois, and more that hadn't even been sown yet. Ethan was on the carpentry detail there.

Every man in camp had been conscripted to some kind of labor. The young bucks, like Shad, were on lumbering crews, or were set to work to provide firewood for the settlement. The older men and boys had been called to ride guard on the stock—all animals of the camp had been turned into one common herd—sheep, cattle, horses, by the thousand. Dan had been ordered to work on the mill and had taken Ethan along, determined that he should learn to build. Even now the clang of hammers reached across to where Corey stood, mingling with the over-all hum of activity that rose from other parts of the new-sprung town. The common striving that had been taught in the families was spread over a whole community.

Trude was looking about her pridefully, with a kind of exultation that sat strangely on her weatherbitten face. Her glance raked the country across the river—those high cliffs that the Indians called Council Bluffs—studded with more sod huts. People moved along the paths leading down to the river edge, hurrying with a purpose. And on this western side of the Missouri a still greater air of enterprise prevailed, for this was where most families were settling. Between the rows of tents heavy lumber wagons crawled, their teams of mules snorting white steam upon the cold air. A crash of logs meant another cabin to begin. Little scrambles of men hurried to lay sod on the roofs of half-finished buildings, while others dug out food cellars. And snowflakes coming faster. . . .

"This is a thing to remember." Sister Trude's voice was hushed with awe. "When gentiles question if you really do have a call from God, remember this." She made a short gesture that took in all of it. "Nobody but those with a call could put up a whole town so fast. Underfed and half of 'em sick, knowing it's going to be a hard winter, yet they don't drift off and try to do better for themselves. We've built a settlement, and it's not even a stake—we've got to leave it, come spring or summer, or whenever we're told. But we'll do it, we'll get to Zion!" She looked up at the sifting sky in solemn rapture. "There's times when you get instructions that don't set well, it's not easy to obey. That's when you've got to think of this—think how it couldn't be done without that word 'obey.' Think how we're not taking orders from Brigham Young, personal, but right straight out of heaven!"

There were times when Corey would have welcomed some instructions from above. Ever since that moment when she and Ethan had ridden along so close together in the darkness and he had ruled her out of his life, she had felt adrift. And somehow sore inside. Much as she told herself she should be glad to be her own mistress again, the truth was that it made a burning in the pit of her heart.

It was some relief to have this new responsibility of keeping Sister Elizabeth's house. It gave her something to come to grips with and kept her from puzzling—at least part of the time. There was plenty to do, to make the bare little room comfortable, even though from the beginning it was the most pleasant of the three cabins.

Hard to say why. Dan had built them all solid and chinked the cracks well. The other two were larger, but of the same outward appearance—windowless log buildings with sod roofs, grouped in a semicircle around the well, which they shared with four other families. However, once inside the homes, the difference became apparent. Sister Trude's was austerely simple. Millie's was a hodgepodge of disorder, with children everywhere. And Sister Elizabeth's was—the warmest.

Her faint perfume rose above the smell of the wood fire on the hearth. The oozing sap of the new log walls was hidden behind her tapestries, and the dirt floor was almost covered by a carpet of a pretty flower pattern. Beside the large fireplace stood the handsome little bedstead. On the table beside it the china shepherdesses flourished and candles burned in a new wooden holder that Dan had whittled.

"This is quite charming," Sister Elizabeth had pronounced, sitting up among her pillows like a small queen. "I think I shall like the wilderness. Are you comfortable, my dear?"

And Corey was—at least so far as her trundle bed in the corner was concerned. The disquiet she felt had more to do with the opposite end of the room, where Ethan's mattress lay on the floor beside a chest which he kept locked. His best suit of clothing hung above it, a spare pair of boots tilted against the wall. More acute was the discovery she had made, in the curtained-off dressing chamber—a box in which he kept his comb and razor and shaving mug. Blushing warmly at sight of these personal objects, Corey had shut the lid in a hurry.

As each constant reminder of his presence seemed to upset her strangely, she tried to outdistance her thoughts by throwing herself into the work of cleaning and cooking and tending Sister Elizabeth's needs. But at night, when the chores were done and supper was on the fire, she caught herself listening for his step outside. When he came in, tired and troubled, she had an overwhelming wish to reach out to him—if just to help as he fumbled to unbutton his coat with cold fingers. And when, without seeming to, he kept his distance from her it began to make Corey ache.

There was nothing to do those long winter evenings but sit quiet and listen, while Ethan and his mother talked of things they had known in the past—play-acting or painted pictures they had seen in England, or the coronation ceremonies which they had once watched, years ago, when Queen Victoria was crowned. It all sounded marvelous to Corey, but it set her a world apart from them. She had to admit she could never speak this sort of language with Ethan.

The only time she could understand him and share his feelings was when the room went still and tense at the sound of Dan's heavy knock on the door. He came almost every evening for a visit with Sister Elizabeth. He would read from the Scriptures, maybe expound on them awhile; then he would invite Sister Elizabeth to serve up a piece of "Paradise Lost" or one of his other favorite poems. It seemed peaceful enough on the surface, but the threat was always just beneath—in the way he would glance at Ethan, the small references he made to "scorners" and "laggards," which he declared were an abomination to the Lord.

Sometimes it blossomed out into a full-blown sermon, after Sister Elizabeth had been put to bed behind her curtains. Any little incident of the workday could provide the text—a nail that Ethan had driven wrong and bent, or a peg that he had cut too short. It all prompted Dan to scathe him, in the name of his eventual salvation. The boy took it without much comment, but after it was over and Dan was gone, Ethan would go off to bed, with hardly a good-night. Corey would hear him twisting around restlessly on his pallet, far into the dark hours.

And then, in early December, there came an evening when Dan arrived in an ominous mood that he didn't try to hide. He always seemed too large for the low-ceilinged room, but that night he overwhelmed it. His shoulders bulked broader, the stride was heavier, the black brows were cocked.

Instead of flipping through the Bible for inspiration, he opened it to a page which he had already marked and launched into the reading, from Proverbs. ". . . train up a child in the way he should go." Corey risked a glance at Ethan; he had gone on polishing his boots, but he was listening, bracing himself almost visibly.

Sister Elizabeth seemed unaware of the tension, and when Dan had finished, she marveled over the beauty of the language. "It reminds me of Polonius," she said. "Let me find that passage—" She was reaching for her book of Shakespeare but Dan stopped her.

"I've a different thought," he said purposefully. "To-night I wish you'd give us the tiger, Sister."

Surprised, but willing, she leaned back against the pillows and looked up at the silken canopy of the bed. It was a short poem, she knew it by heart. In a delicate, beautiful tone of mystery, she recited: " '*Tiger, tiger, burning bright, in the forests of the night. . . .*' " And when she came to the line, "*Did He who made the lamb, make thee?*" Dan slapped his knee in gloomy approval. After the poem was finished, he stood up to give them his prayer and blessing. Corey and Ethan came dutifully to stand beside the bed.

"Lord"—Dan's eyes were squinted tight shut, his hands locked in front of him—"you reared up a good man in that poet, who wrote so true as to how you made the tiger and the lamb, too. You made a whole slew of critters, and they're all good for something. We know we can't all be tigers or poets or carpenters. The main thing is to find out what we *are* good at and do it. So, help those that are muddleheaded—and you know who I mean—to strive harder to serve you, and help the rest of us to lead 'em into thy ways. Amen. God bless the family."

He opened his eyes and fixed Ethan with a look which the boy returned warily. For the first time Sister Elizabeth seemed disturbed. Hands still clasped, she glanced from one to the other of them anxiously. Ethan stepped forward to brush her cheek with a kiss.

"You're tired, Mother. It's time for us all to say good night. Let me draw the curtains for you."

Dan paced away, over to the hearth. When Corey followed, he glanced down at her somberly. "You'd best get to bed, daughter. What talk I must have with the boy is beyond a woman to understand."

She trembled to argue with him, but she couldn't desert Ethan now. "Please, sir, I must—I should set the bread to rise."

"Then do it," he agreed reluctantly. "You're a good lass, but even the best females are born weak. They need a man to lean on, and I aim to see you get proper support."

Corey had private doubts as to the relative weakness of her sex, but she kept them to herself as she busied about starting the bread. When Ethan had settled his mother he came over to join them.

There was an indefinable change in him, a trace of daring as he said, "Very well, Dan. What have I done now?"

Tanner shot him a glance as if surprised at the challenge. "I didn't come to badger you, son. You've been trying your best, I reckon, though it's hard for me to see how you could still be so hapless at the work. The master carpenter at the mill convinced me today you'll never learn to handle a hatchet."

"Yes, sir," Ethan said, "I could have advised you of that some months ago."

Dan's look darkened but he held his temper. "I can see now that it's wasteful for you to spend any more time at it, and waste's a sin, especially these days. So the question is: what sort of trade *can* you learn? Do you have any notions? I'll be willing to listen to 'em."

"I'm giving it a good deal of consideration," Ethan told him dryly.

"You're a great one to moon around. There's a certain other matter, too, that you've still not made up your mind about." Dan spoke with some hidden meaning that they both understood, but he didn't press it. "I don't want to judge you, boy—the Lord made you naturally slow. But there comes a time to cut a horse from the herd and ride it. If you've got even half an idea, lay it on the table. Maybe we can help you figure it out."

Ethan's chin set hard. "It seems to me that a man's confusion should be his own private property."

Dan's face reddened with anger. "If you won't make your own move, I'll have to do it for you. There's one thing I've seen you do well, and that's mend harness. You kept your leather in good shape all across Iowa. So, come tomorrow, I aim to take you down to the cobbler's and apprentice you. The world's always going to need boots. It's a good trade."

"It is," Ethan agreed coldly, "but not for me. No, wait, Dan—I've seen this coming longer than you have. I've made inquiries and found there's one kind of worker badly needed, with illness beginning to take off more and more people. So I've applied to the Council and received permission to take a place on the burial crews."

Corey caught her breath and even Dan looked confounded. It was the hardest labor of the camp and the dreariest—digging graves out of the frozen prairie. It was true, of course, that the job needed doing and for certain not many wanted it.

Dan scowled. "I don't like it. Those men are the poorest learnt, the sorriest of our brothers. Only the dullards get put to that work—I'd mislike to see a member of my family there. What's more, it won't fit you for the time to come when you'll have your own family to clothe and feed."

"When that need arises, I'll meet it," Ethan said steadily. "For now my only duty is to serve the community—you told me that yourself. And I'll serve, Dan. I'll contribute my back muscle. But no man can tell me what profession to put my mind to. And no man shall."

Eleven

It had made Corey glad, when Ethan won the encounter with Dan. For a few minutes he'd stood so firm. But in the days that followed he seemed more subdued than ever, as if the hidden trouble which had shadowed him all this while was deepening, as subtly as winter settling in. While he still tried to carry on light conversation with his mother these evenings, he was distracted. And as soon as she had retired he would pace over to the hearth and slump down before the fire.

When at first Corey came to sit beside him quietly he hardly appeared to notice. But gradually he came to expect it, even to take some comfort in it, she thought. Sometimes they would sink into a long silence broken only by the crackle of the embers. At other times he would come out with abrupt questions–about her early life, how she grew up, and what her father had taught her concerning this or that. When she told him, he would listen as if he were trying to fit her answers into some problem of his own. Sometimes, absently, he rubbed at the back of his neck, as if to loosen the tightness of fatigue, though he never spoke of how hard this new bleak work was.

Once she dared ask the question, "Do you take satisfaction in the–the–job you're doing?"

Ethan stared at her, startled. "I detest it, more than anything I've ever had to do."

"Then why–?"

"Because I got tired of being called a shirker. Digging is something I can do, something Dan can't argue about. He can't accuse me of being useless; the Lord knows there are more burials every day. This fever is spreading badly. The children–" With one of those sudden violent gestures he kicked the stool back and stood up, to roam about the room. Corey shivered at the thought of those small graves.

"Could it have been worse, working with the cobbler?"

Ethan came to a halt in front of her, his hands shoved deep in his pockets. "In my lexicon, it would be a sin to let a man teach me his craft when I've no intention of following it. But aside from that, there comes a time when you have to establish the fact that you're independent. Don't you? At least for me there are certain matters too personal to be dictated by Brigham Young, or anyone else." Abruptly he put a hand on her shoulder in a brotherly gesture of apology. "I'm sorry—I'm just confusing you, and that's another sin in my own 'golden book.' Good night, Corey."

After that time she had to live with another secret—one which only dawned on her slowly—that Ethan was not really a very firm Mormon. Worse yet, the ring of his words had stirred an uncertainty in her, calling up some of her own earlier doubts—the questions she used to ask Pa long ago in those days when she had first begun to reason and understand things. Whenever she felt the perplexity wakening in her, Corey said her prayers in a hurry.

She was hard at them one day late in December when she was startled by a small crash out behind the cabin—for a confused moment she thought she must have whispered something that offended the Lord. Then common sense set in—she realized it was just Shad bringing the firewood and got up off her knees hastily.

Whenever he came over he tried to invite himself inside—to warm up, he said, though there was a perfectly good fire in his own house not thirty feet away. And once past the door, he was difficult—flirty toward her, a little swaggering toward Sister Elizabeth, who always seemed upset by him. So Corey usually tried to intercept him and keep him outside.

Today he was waiting for her out in back; he could make no good case of being frozen, for it was a mild afternoon—the sun was spreading a thin warmth over the snow-crusted hills.

"More like April than Christmas Eve." Shad stretched lazily. "A fine afternoon to be let off work. Especially if a man's got company to spend it with."

"Were all the workers dismissed early?" Instinctively Corey glanced toward the rising land behind the settlement.

Shad laughed. "We were, and that's a fact. But don't expect your gentleman gravedigger home soon. As I drove back to town with my last load, I saw Brother Ethan walking out across the prairies—toward the sunset." He made an airy motion with an aloof look, meant to mock Ethan's manner. "So you'd best settle for somebody who knows where he's at. The band's gathering over near the Council House—will you walk down there with me?"

"Certainly not," she told him flatly. "It's not even proper you should ask."

"We could make it proper," he said blandly. "It wouldn't take much to convince Dan that there's a mistake been made. If you were to say one word, he'd call off this wedding. Then you could pick a proper man."

"You?" She half wanted to laugh, but sensed that beneath the light tone he was serious.

Shad nodded judiciously. "I've been watching you. You're a good worker and healthy—half the womenfolk in this camp got the chills and shakes. You're sturdy enough to mother a fine crop of young'uns. I'd take you to wife if you was willing."

Corey bent over and began to pick up some firewood. "Thank you. No."

Shad circled her suspiciously, then suddenly caught her arm and drew her up straight to face him. "You're laughing."

"No, I'm not. But it's a strange way to propose—you never mentioned love."

He dismissed that impatiently. "You're no winsome sort, to put store by such. You're not in love with that thin-blooded Britisher. What is it, then? How come you to turn down a hardy man like me?"

Corey broke loose from the bruising grip of his fingers. Tartly she said, "Because you've got a way of figuring things wrong—to think you're such a charmer, to think I'd break my vows. You're even wrong about Ethan. Yonder he comes now."

At sight of the man tramping down the road from the heights, Shad's handsome young face reddened and he turned on his heel, walking away fast. For an instant Corey regretted the cutting edge of her tone, but not the words. Shad was too well favored for his own good; if he could lose some of that blundering conceit, he'd likely make a fair mate for some girl—

And then she forgot all about him as she watched Ethan coming, striding along faster than usual, casting a long-legged shadow ahead of him. When he lifted a hand in a small gesture of greeting, Corey's heart stumbled inside her and went to beating an uneven skip-time.

When he was still a hundred yards away she could

sense a lightness of spirit about him. As he came up, he was smiling.

"You're early." She welcomed him warmly.

"No, actually I'm late. There were no burials today, thank God, and we were sent off an hour ago. But I thought"—he reached in the knapsack he carried and brought forth a rabbit, fresh-killed and cleaned, ready for the pan—"I thought we should have something special for Christmas dinner tomorrow. Now if we only had the making of a plum pudding. . . ."

That afternoon, as they all sat together and Ethan warmed his hands by the fire, he and Sister Elizabeth told Corey what a time Christmas always was in England—how the Cathedral bells always rang, how there was dancing and holly and roast goose. Once Ethan laughed aloud when his mother called to mind the time he, as a small boy, had been forced to don a costume and entertain guests with a rendition of some song.

"How I detested that lace collar and velvet hat!" He shook his head; then on impulse, he sang, in a deep, true voice:

"On the first day of Christmas
My true love sent to me
A partridge in a pear tree—

and I must say I'd be glad to have a brace of the birds for our dinner tomorrow."

"Oh, no, the hare will be more of a delight," his

mother insisted. "I can hardly wait."

It was such a comfortable feeling, to sit quiet and watch them enjoying themselves, that Corey was almost resentful when someone tapped at the door. It was Lucy, standing outside in the early dusk.

"I thought you might like to know—the band is gathering to play hymns. Of course you may not want to leave that fire. It's turning cold out."

"Come in." Ethan held the door for her. "Is Sister Trude with you?"

"No, Mama's home with a touch of colic. I've got the sniffles myself, but I do love to hear the band play. If you don't care to come, I'd not blame you, but I think I'll go along." There was a wistfulness about the words.

Ethan spoke quickly. "Of course we'll join you. Mother—you'll be all right alone for a while?"

Sister Elizabeth nodded with perfect understanding. "Go on, my dears."

And so the three of them walked out through the big encampment, Ethan with a girl tucked close on either arm, while from the square ahead came the strains of the music, which had already begun. They were playing "By the Rivers of Babylon"—Corey thought she had never heard any sound so lovely and melancholy, drifting down to them on the quiet crystalline air.

Surely no one could doubt that the Prophet had been gifted with holy vision, to bring this band clear from

England years ago. They said it had been a mighty job, converting the whole lot of them at once. Who but a prophet would have guessed how badly they would be needed, out here on the verge of this wild country, to put spirit into a frostbitten homeless lot of people? She had a mind to mention it to Ethan, but there was no time now, as they reached the outskirts of the crowd.

It was a fair gathering, though many of the Saints looked chilled and ailing. Scattered among them were a number of Indians—the handsome Omahas who had loaned them this land on which they had built. Solemn and silent, they were great ones to attend any sort of meeting, and stood around now, crowned by their feathery finery, listening gravely while the band struck up a chorus of "The Upper California, oh, that's the land for me!" and the crowd joined in, their voices shivery but fervent.

Corey heard a familiar booming tone and glanced around to see Shad standing not far away. Meg was clinging to his arm; there was triumph in her smile as she joined in the song.

"I swear I'd sing, too, if my throat wasn't so raw," Lucy remarked cheerfully.

The girl standing next to her leaned over and whispered. "You missed the best part of all. Brother Brigham spoke a blessing to open the concert."

Corey was disappointed to have missed that; she had never seen the president of the Council. But now the band had switched to a different kind of tune and she was arrested by it—a strange, fluting, sprightly music that was so joyous, Corey hardly understood why it made her feel misty-eyed. Glancing at Ethan, she saw that it affected him, too.

"Do you like that?" he asked softly. "It's Handel's Water Music." And she glimpsed the full measure of his homesickness—for a moment Ethan wasn't hiding anything from her.

"He's nearly himself again!" Sister Elizabeth marveled that next morning as soon as she and Corey were alone. Ethan had gone off early, vowing to get them a Yule log—whatever that was. "It's a special log for the Christmas fire," his mother explained. "We should have brought it in last evening, to be quite correct."

"Do they grow along the Missouri?" Corey asked doubtfully.

Sister Elizabeth laughed. "Oak will do—or any good wood that will burn a long while. The specialness is in the tradition. In our household, the man of the family always chops it down himself."

Which was a piece of luck! It meant they would have *hours* before he would be back. Corey began to roll up her sleeves.

"Then we have time to make this plum pudding he's so wishing for. What do we need? How do we do it?"

Like conspirators, they rushed to work. Sister Elizabeth sat up amid her comforters and mixed it—flour up to her elbows and an elfin delight on her small face. As she called for the ingredients Corey went in search of them. A lump of suet from Sister Trude's larder of special delicacies. Millie had a box of spices. Lucy provided the plums—some that she had dried way back on Sugar Creek. Corey herself had gathered walnuts as they went along the trail. And at the last minute Sarah and Samantha came over with an offer from their own precious stock of dried wild cherries, so that the pudding would have "raisins."

"Sweet children!" Sister Elizabeth exclaimed. "We'll give them each a piece later. Now hurry—into the pudding bag with it." They managed to have it shut away tight in the oven by the time Ethan returned, so that he didn't suspect, though he did sniff curiously as he brought the big log over on his shoulder and set it on the hearth.

By then Corey was busy with the rabbit, and the air was full of the smell of gravy and roasting potatoes. "Sister Trude would be scandalized because I didn't boil them," she admitted. "And we may starve next month, because I've used up all of January's carrots. I guess I'll never make a manager."

"Better to be a poet!" Sister Elizabeth cried gayly. "That dinner has the symmetry of a sonnet. I do believe I feel well enough to come to table with you."

When they were gathered around Ethan offered grace in his shy way, a simple-spoken gratitude for the day, the meal, for their health and company together. Then, with quiet enjoyment, he set about serving up the "hare." And if there was one thing Corey had cooked plenty of, it was cottontail rabbit. She was gratified by the way they savored it, though for some reason she could hardly eat. Too excited. Or pricked by some foreboding, as if they were snatching these few moments of closeness under the shadow of distress.

But the mood was forgotten at sight of Ethan's face when she brought forth the pudding. As she set the steaming, fragrant dish before him he stared from it to her as if this were all some piece of magic. Corey thought she could have explained how it was done—how everyone had given to it—and she would, after a while. But for the moment she let him marvel. She was just glad that Ethan could believe—at least in small miracles.

Twelve

"Just between you and me," Lucy whispered hoarsely, "Ethan is not exactly a Mormon at all." She and Corey were sitting before the fire one evening in January, talking guardedly so as not to waken Sister Elizabeth who was ailing and had retired early. Illness was raging through the camp these days. Trude and Millie both had the fever, and Lucy herself was flushed—the rasp in her throat sounded painful. "Fact is, Ethan's never been baptized."

Corey tried not to look too shocked. "Doesn't Dan take that amiss?"

"Gracious, yes!" Lucy glanced toward the big bed where the curtains were drawn tight. "Papa and Sister Elizabeth worked on him hard those first months after he came to this country with them, but he just kept saying he had to think it over. He said he couldn't bring himself to feel like a saint. I don't see why. It's a mighty comfort, when Satan gets to plucking at you. I tried to explain it to Ethan once, but questions–!" She made a fretful gesture. "You never heard the like. He wanted to know if anybody beside the Prophet ever really saw the golden plates."

Corey thought back guiltily to the time when she had plagued Pa about that very thing, long ago when he was first giving her Church instruction. He'd explained how, naturally, you take a prophet's word for these things.

"And when I told Ethan we were all descended from the original tribes of Israel he kept arguing–arguing–" Lucy broke off again, coughing convulsively. "Said we couldn't be, because we aren't Hebrews. The Lamanites–he doubted the Lamanites, too. Kept saying the Bible never mentioned any people from Israel who had red skins."

Corey smiled a little. Even Pa had trouble remembering to call the red men "Lamanites"; he still slipped once in a while and called them "Injuns."

"I *told* him," Lucy went on thinly, "how it's all in the Book of Mormon, and that *is* the Bible. Ethan's such a quiet man–you'd never dream he could be so stubborn. . . ." Another spell of coughing racked her, and she clutched at her throat, wincing.

Corey set a log on the fire and hung the kettle over the blaze. "I'll make you some tea." She was growing disturbed by the high color in the girl's face, the way she rambled along, as though she were a bit lightheaded. "I doubt you should have come out in this cold."

"I had to get away from the house," Lucy murmured painfully. "Meg's taken over the fireplace—Shad's courting her every evening these days. Just between you and me, old Satan's trying to tempt me to be jealous."

Impulsively Corey reached across and laid a hand on Lucy's. "You'll find somebody better than Shad."

The older girl smiled wearily. "The only man who ever was kind to me was Ethan. He's too young, and anyway he's yours. But Corey, please—help him. He grew up different from us. In his country there were sinful things—tobacco and spirits—! His folks used to put brandy on those plum puddings of theirs. You didn't know that—" Lucy choked and swallowed. "It's not his fault, but you must help him come into the faith, and soon. Before Papa loses patience. I heard him talking the other day—what he's going to do if—" Her voice cracked, she was taken by a hard spasm of coughing, and started to her feet. "Can't . . . breathe . . ."

Corey leaped to her side in alarm. "Come—lie down."

Lucy stared at her in wide-eyed panic, a terrible little strangulated noise coming from her throat. Corey urged her over to Ethan's pallet which was nearest, but she broke away and turned wildly, as if to run to the door. Her face was livid, her eyes strained—and then the sense dimmed out of them and she pitched forward. Corey caught her and eased her down onto the mattress.

Frantically she chafed her wrists, opened the throat of her dress. *So lifeless . . . but what can I do? I've got to get help!*

Scrambling up, she ran to the door and jerked it open. Out in the twilight a familiar figure was trudging across the snow toward the cabin. She rushed to meet him.

"Ethan, come quickly! Lucy got to choking and fainted. I don't think she's breathing!"

Ethan had already broken into a run. As he reached the cabin door he bent and scooped up some snow, then hurried in and over to the side of the stricken girl. Her skin was deathly gray now, her mouth ajar. Ethan pressed the snow to her throat, holding it there with one hand while with the other he felt for her pulse.

"A cup of hot water. Hurry!"

Corey hastened to comply. When she brought it to him he had unlocked the chest beside his bed. Taking out a bottle, he poured a few drops of some aromatic liquid into the water—strong fumes rose from it. Carefully he held the cup where Lucy could inhale the steam. She had begun to gasp, slowly; the terrible congestion was fading from her face though she was still unconscious. Ethan beckoned Corey.

"Stay beside her, keep holding the cup where she can breathe the vapor." He stood up and began to strip off his coat and roll up his sleeves. Corey's hands were trembling as she held the cup and watched that motionless figure struggling to draw each shallow breath.

"She has a badly infected throat—I've thought so for

a week." Ethan sounded angry as he rummaged in the chest and brought out a whole handful of bottles, which he carried to the table. "Damnable, to watch someone sicken and be powerless to help. Where do you keep the wheat meal?"

"In the teabox on the shelf."

He got it and the kettle and began to mix a paste in a cup, adding this and that from the bottles, then spread the mixture on a clean towel and brought it over to the bedside. Brushing the last snow aside, he applied the compress to Lucy's throat.

"What is that?" Corey asked in a hushed voice.

"Just a poultice made of simple, natural materials," he said defiantly. "I know it probably seems wicked to you, to resort to such an evil thing as medication."

She didn't answer. She was thinking that, faith or no faith, Lucy was hardly in a position right now to employ prayers to relieve her trouble.

"What shall I do?" she whispered.

"You could add some more hot water to your cup."

She went to get the kettle. From the steam the pungent odors were as strong as before. Returning to Lucy's side with it, she asked curiously, "What did you put in this?"

"Better that you not know."

Corey watched him silently a minute, thinking back. "That day you stayed at the landing, you were doing this? Treating those miserable people with—cures?"

Tightly he said, "If you see men lying in agony you

give them something to ease the pain, if you have it. When you know a festering sore will turn gangrenous, you don't walk off and forget it. Not if you want to sleep of nights."

"You can pray—" she began.

"Yes, that, too!" he snapped. "But no prayer is going to cauterize a bullet wound or set a broken bone."

Lucy had begun to stir a little. Her eyelids fluttered and she blinked at them, bewildered. "What happened to me?" she asked in a weak voice.

Gently Ethan answered, "Nothing to be alarmed over. You had a little fainting spell. Lie still and try not to excite yourself."

"My throat closed up," she murmured, as the memory came back. Then becoming aware of the poultice, she struggled to sit up, pushing it aside. "You know that's forbidden!"

He smiled patiently. "Whatever you say. But please—don't upset yourself. We don't want you to have another coughing spell."

Lucy was staring at the cup that Corey held. "You're helping him!" She began to sound distraught and the flush came up in her cheeks.

"This is just hot water, Lu," Corey found herself lying swiftly.

"I'm going home." Lucy began to button the collar of her dress with unsteady fingers. Corey helped her, noticing how pink her throat was where the application had lain. Ethan had gone to get her cloak; now he wrapped it about her and picked her up in his arms against her protests.

"I can walk—!"

"Now then, you know I'm not really old Nick, come to whisk you off to the bad place," he told her in much the same teasing tone he used to soothe his mother when she grew alarmed. As he carried her out he was saying lightly, "You'd best stay in bed till your fever goes down. Drink warm broth with plenty of salt in it—not too hot—"

Corey closed the door behind them. Going back to the table, she picked up the bottles curiously. Oil of Camphor . . . Oil of Eucalyptus . . . Oil of Mustard Seed . . . She and Pa had eaten wild mustard greens many a time and she used mustard in the cooking. She wondered if this was seed of the same plant. And if it was, could it be so wrong to use it on Lucy's throat? Ethan certainly had no doubts—the way he had moved as he blended them, surely, with such purpose. He'd been like a stranger, steady, decisive.

And yet when he let himself back into the room a few minutes later the briskness was gone. He seemed more unhappy than ever. Going to his mother's bedside, he glanced in on her, then drew the curtains tight again before coming to the table. For a minute he stood facing Corey silently.

"You helped—you even lied. I'm leading you into bad habits," he said.

She shook her head. It couldn't have been a sin, to

bring Lucy out of that terrible seizure. "Pa wouldn't think so. He believes in praying, but he never was against such a thing as bone setting. Or this. He'd not say it was wicked, to help her breathe again! It was mostly potions he said were wrong."

Ethan went over and poured a cup full of tea. Coming back, he handed it to her. "You look a bit pale—you've had quite a fright."

Gratefully Corey drank it while he watched, with a slight embittered smile. "And that," he added, "is a potion."

Corey set the cup down sharply. "What did you put in it?"

"Nothing. Tea is a natural stimulant." He gathered up the bottles and took them back to the chest. Following, Corey saw that it contained more vials and flasks, books and instruments—knives, pincers, scissors, strange gleaming tools that frightened her.

"Do you—do things with those?" she ventured.

"No. I've not had the training. I had only time to learn a little—precious little—from my father before he died. That finished it for good." He shut the lid abruptly and snapped the lock.

"Those things were his?"

Ethan nodded. "He was a physician—a fine one."

Something fitted in place in Corey's mind. "Dr. Drake!"

"Yes. I imagine you've heard Mother call out for him. She was very dependent upon him. It was when he died that her—mind—began to wander at times. That's why she needs me near, and yet—" Ethan sat down before the fire, his head in his hands.

Corey took the low stool close beside him. Right or wrong she would have given anything to bring back that self-possession he had shown for a few minutes. When he just sat there, hunched over and lost in some grim thought, she risked a hand on his knee. Ethan started, as if he'd forgotten her presence.

"I'm sorry. I have no right to wish my problems onto you," he said, "but it's only fair to tell you what's going to happen. I've been trying to shake it off ever since we came to these pestiferous bottoms, but it's driven home every time I glance around. Fever—lung congestion—children with canker sores and croup, dying—how could anyone shut it out of mind? I don't have many remedies and even less skill, but I've got to go around to them and try to help however best I can —as much as they'll let me do. Not all of them are so rigidly against treatment as Dan is."

"But if he hears of it—!"

"And there's the danger. He has threatened before to turn me out of the family. I don't know whether he would—he knows how Mother gets at times. But he could. And then there's you to think of—you've been humiliated enough on my account. So you see, I'm not unaware or indifferent to the consequences. And yet I've got to go ahead—I can't explain it, Corey. It's something that puts a grip on me. It forces me even to break a vow I made myself—that I'd never touch anything in that chest again."

The whole confession poured forth like flood water over a broken levee—he must have been needing to talk for so long. Tenderly Corey took his hand in both of hers.

"But if it means so much to you, Ethan, why have you vowed against it?"

"Because—" he seemed to flounder over the question. With an effort he regained his composure; remotely he answered, "Because there's no room in the profession for cowards."

Thirteen

"When you start wanting to weave cloth," Millie said, "you're beginning to feel like a wife."

"Yes'm," Corey agreed, though privately she knew her feelings were more nearly the opposite. It was the very uncertainty which had caused her to ask for the loom to be set up in her cabin. Now as the two of them finished tying on the warp, she just hoped the work would keep her fingers busy, even if it couldn't entirely absorb her worries.

"I can remember," Millie was going on, "when I wove my first piece of homespun. I was only about your age—I made a whole suit of clothes for my man—my first husband, Shad's father. He was so proud of it—and the yarn wasn't even dyed." Prattling along, she tightened the roller so that the threads were taut. "This is a good blue—it will look fine on Ethan, after those dark British clothes. And it'll be warm—we spun the yarn extra heavy last spring. Seemed likely someone would need it this winter. My, it's been a hard season."

And yet Millie had stood the bleak months of January and February better than most. She had lost some of her plumpness, and her eyes had traces of shadow beneath them, but they were warm and pleased with the chance to show someone a skill she was good at herself.

"Now set your feet on the treadles—put the left one down first. See, this is the shed you weave through. Throw your shuttle, pack the thread with the beater. Now put the right foot down and you've made your second shed. You work up a rhythm after a while."

"Thank you, Sister," Corey said. "May I make you a pot of tea?"

"No, I must go back to the children. Sammy's still in bed and Saul and Staley both just up. I doubt if the girls can keep them quiet as they should be. My, I'll be glad when they can all go back to school, and yet I'm afraid to send them. There's still so much sickness around." She glanced toward Sister Elizabeth's bed. "I should look in on her. I haven't been real neighborly since we got here. I'm ashamed I haven't been over oftener since she's been took down."

"She's feeling better," Corey said in a low voice, "but she still sleeps most of the time. When she keeps the curtains closed I don't disturb her."

"I was afraid she'd never bear up under this hard life.

She was frail, even when Dan brought her from England. He converted her, you know. It's wonderful how the spirit will carry a body through." Millie spoke with a gravity that went deeper than Corey would have expected. "Ethan's the one I worry for most," she added. "He hasn't had the call yet."

"I know," Corey said uneasily.

"He seems so lonely." Millie's look was soft with kindness. "How soon do you turn sixteen?"

Realizing the import of the question, Corey blushed. "Not till next September."

"I wish it were sooner. That young man needs a woman's warmth."

"He's almighty hard to comfort," Corey said evasively, thinking sorely of how Ethan had denied her that right, all those long months ago. But even if the betrothal were real, she thought she wouldn't have known how to help him. "I can't even get him to eat much these days."

"Food!" Millie tossed her brown curls indignantly. "Oh, I know, some women'll tell you a man's whole welfare is in his stomach. But I know better. They need a smile and soft arms around them, somebody who'll be a mite foolish; it makes them feel wonderful wise. Mainly they need love—a lot of it. You can't do much yet; it would seem forward. But if a time comes—I don't know why, but I feel something hanging over Ethan—when you see the need to hold him hard in the midst of some trouble, then do it."

But how? If he won't let you? Later that evening, when Corey was alone, she kept hearing the words like a portent of disaster. Hold on to him? Everything in her was stretching out to do that, but he was a million miles away. *He thinks of me as a backwoods hobbledehoy*—Corey shot the shuttle through the shed. *For all he seems to scorn himself, if he were to think of marrying someone, it would be a gentle lady like his mother.* Her hand moved jerkily, and the shuttle leaped back across the warp. *He hardly even talks to me*—

Even though they were silent partners in a grim game, Ethan never spoke of it, nor did she. These nights, after supper, when he filled his knapsack with medications from the chest and went out into the darkness, she knew what he was about and he knew that she knew, but they didn't discuss it. He never asked her to conceal his whereabouts, but she did.

Fortunately Dan's visits were short these days. As a deacon he was much in demand to pray over the ailing. He went among them every evening, to read from the Bible, to lay hands on them. To try to help heal them he worked as seriously as Ethan did. It was just luck that the two hadn't met over some sickbed.

Corey fingered the few inches of cloth she had woven, thinking of how the threads packed tight, criss and cross, against each other—too tight to see through. Something like that was happening inside her—Pa and Dan and all the Saints believing one way and Ethan, another.

When she heard him outside, stamping the snow from his boots, Corey got up quickly to open the door. He was earlier than usual—as he came in she went ahead of him to the fire.

"I'm sorry I don't have the tea made—"

"Never mind, I won't be here long. I must make a trip, and the sooner I get started the better. I'll need to borrow your mare. I've already taken her from the herd —she's tied just outside. I thought you'd not mind."

"Tonight? You're going somewhere tonight?"

He nodded. "I only came back here to tell you. And to see Mother once more."

"But where? For how long?"

Hesitating, he studied her as if undecided. "Wouldn't you prefer not to know about it so that you can say quite truthfully that you've no idea where I have gone?"

"No! Please, tell me!"

"If you ask it, then I must, because I need a favor from you. Rather a large one, I'm afraid. Just a moment." He went over quietly to his mother's bed and bent over the sleeping woman.

While she waited, Corey got out a loaf of fresh bread and sliced it, spreading the layers with lard, some with jelly. And there was a bit of cheese she had been saving. She wrapped the loaf in a piece of oilcloth and opened his knapsack. It was full of bottles—most of them empty.

"Just leave them in there," he said, coming back to

her side. "I'll dispose of them out on the trail somewhere; it will be just that much less for Dan to discover. If he ever gets curious about that chest of mine, I'm done for."

"Has he begun to suspect? Is that why—?"

Ethan shook his head. He had taken the double-barreled pistol out to check its priming. "My stock of medicines is about gone. I'm going to get more."

"Going—where?"

"To the nearest settlement."

"But that's a hundred and fifty miles from here. In *Missouri!*"

He shoved the gun back into his belt, buttoning his shirt over it again. "I'll try to be back in four or five days—it's possible my absence won't be missed. The other men on the burial crew will think I've taken down sick; they know I've had a congestion of the head coming on for a week or more. If anyone does ask, though, please say you've no notion where I've gone or why. Let me do the explaining when I get back."

"But where will you sleep?"

"Wherever I am when the need comes over me." He spoke impatiently. "Right now I must be on my way. Don't argue, Corey. There are people out there dying. One woman tonight—if I'd just had some remedy—I didn't know what to do for her. The life slipped out of her while I watched." She glimpsed the torment in his look. "So I decided to go down to St. Joseph. There must be some kind of doctor there."

"But if you tell him where you've come from, they may lynch you. Or jail you—"

"I'll take the chance. I've got to go on with what I've started—there are some curatives that need to be repeated to be effective."

Anxiously Corey asked, "Do the people accept your doctoring? Don't they feel, as Dan does, that it's wrong?"

"Some do. And I can't argue with them. I know of no reference to castor oil in the Bible, which is the only authority they recognize. The truth is, many have been abused at the hands of quacks, in earlier days before they became Mormons, and I can't blame them for being suspicious. The younger people are more willing to concede that the bark and roots and flowers of certain plants may have been created by the Lord on purpose to heal. If I can convince them of that, I can sometimes help them. But there are so many things I don't have knowledge of, myself." He shook his head. "These sores on the children—the black canker—it doesn't respond to sulphur or saleratus baths or anything else I've tried. That's why I'm going to get some advice." He buckled on the knapsack.

Corey bit back the words of protest that rose like a cry of fear. Instead, she said, "What is it you want of me—this favor you spoke of?"

Ethan beckoned her over to his mother's bedside. "If she grows overwrought while I'm gone you must quiet her. It isn't just a matter of kindness, but necessity.

There's so little strength in that fragile body, she mustn't burn it up in undue excitement. And so–" He reached up to one of the pieces of ornate carving on the canopy and twisted it; it came off in his hand to reveal a compartment. Inside were several paper packets. He took one out and unfolded it to show her the contents, a white powder. "Half of one of these will serve to lull her. A whole dose will send her off to sleep for twelve hours and keep her quiet another twenty-four."

"I thought–" Corey stared up at him. "What was that bottle Dan took away from you?"

"Water. I kept it there on purpose for such an event. I regret"–Ethan sounded wry–"to have to admit my skulduggery this way. You'll think for certain I am the Devil's disciple and am trying to enlist you in the same service. But if you'll help me this once, I'll not ask another sacrifice of you." He folded the paper of powder and restored it to its hiding place. "Will you do this much for me?"

For an instant Corey wondered if a refusal might not keep him from this dangerous trip. And then he turned to face her and there were no barriers between them. It was so much the way she had hoped he might look at her someday that she couldn't disappoint him.

"I will," she said.

In those days that followed Corey often wondered if Ethan knew how much he had asked. Between her fear for his safety and anxiety as to what would happen if his absence were discovered, she could hardly eat, much less sleep. She stayed inside the house as much as possible to avoid chance encounters with the rest of the family, but it was a restless vigil. As the fourth day passed, the waiting began to twist her tight inside, and by the afternoon of the fifth she was taut as a fiddle-string.

That evening she tried to read a little poetry to Sister Elizabeth, not caring much what it was about. All these fancy sonnets had references to Greek goddesses with unpronounceable names, flowery love expressed in too much language. She understood what it meant, but it could have been said so much more simply. Sister Elizabeth relished it, though, lying back against her pillows with her eyes closed, smiling faintly. Once she looked over at Corey dreamily.

"You're reading with real emotion tonight, my dear."

Strangely, she seemed unconcerned—or possibly not quite aware of Ethan's long absence. Corey had been able to satisfy her with excuses; she seemed to be living half in another world. Corey envied her. As she read on, her voice filling the cabin, all the while her listening was bent toward the snowy world beyond its walls.

When Sister Elizabeth wearied finally, Corey brushed her hair and gave her a last cup of warm milk, then drew the bed curtains and the cabin became full of an echoing stillness. Somewhere outside the crisp crunch of boots on the snow made her hold her breath. Not Ethan—they came too heavily.

A tap on the door and the latch lifted before she could answer. Dan came in—one look at his face told her that he'd found out something. He looked at the loom, then around the empty room. At the curtained bed.

"She's asleep?"

"Yes, sir. Just barely."

He came over to the hearth, the big shoulders swinging. "How long has the boy been gone?"

Some intuition told Corey that he already knew. "More than four days," she answered shakily.

"Why didn't you tell me?"

"He asked me not to speak of it. Whatever it is, he counted it important."

Dan stood with his hands locked behind him. "I've just learned that he took your mare from the herd. Nobody's seen him. I scarce believed it. His mother—he'd not leave her."

"He'll be back. I know he'll come back—"

Dan muttered, "If he didn't, I'd near be glad. I've tried my best, the Lord knows, but I can't see any spirit growing in him. I'm sorry, lass. I'm sorry your father made a poor choice for you."

Corey was about to protest that, then they both held still, listening. Corey's heart jumped fearfully, for this time she knew it was Ethan's step outside. The latch raised quietly and he let himself in. After an instant's surprise he came over to them stiffly, moving as if he were exhausted to the core—unshaven and spattered. The knapsack was missing.

Dan looked him up and down. "Well?"

Slowly Ethan drew off his gloves and held his hands out to the dying fire. His fingers were white with cold.

"Speak out, boy!" Dan ordered fiercely.

"Yes, sir. What shall I say?"

"Hellfire and damnation! I want to know where you've been."

"Out on the prairie." Ethan spoke between clenched teeth. He was beginning to shudder with returning warmth. "I had to go away for a while—to think. About what I'm going to do. About what's worth living for and what isn't." Wrung out of him this way, it sounded like the truth.

"You *thought?* For four–five days?" Dan sounded incredulous.

"It wasn't long enough."

"Meaning you still don't know."

"No, sir."

"And this is all the excuse you have?"

Ethan looked at him wearily. "Do I need an excuse? Isn't this what they did in olden Bible times—go into the wilderness with their problems? Isn't it allowed any more?"

"They came back with answers, too. What did you come home with?"

Ethan shook his head. "I can't say yet."

For a while the two of them stood silent, elbow to elbow, staring into the last flames that licked along the embers. Corey held her breath, afraid to move lest it send things off the wrong way. At last Dan slapped a fist in his palm.

"I've near had enough. I'll advise you this much, son: ponder good over what you have in mind, but do it soon." With a curt nod to Corey he went out.

She waited until the door latch fell, then caught Ethan's arm in both hands. "Thank God you're safe!"

He moved away, lowering himself into a chair and leaning forward to catch the heat from the glowing coals. When she moved to put another log on, he stopped her.

"I'm going to bed at once. I've not lain down in twenty-four hours."

"Did you get what you went for?"

He nodded, but there was small satisfaction in it. "I cached the supplies before coming home. I thought Dan might be waiting here for me. How did Mother fare in my absence?"

"She rested quiet the whole time."

"Thank God." But he still sounded depressed.

"Did you run into any trouble?" she asked. For it was evident something had happened.

"You might say so. As I told Dan—I thought. Too much."

Impulsively she put an arm around his shoulders. Ethan started up out of his seat as if it were a trap.

"Are you trying to torment me?" he demanded, then wheeled away from her to go into the dressing room. She heard him kick his boots off—one of them banged against the wall with a fury.

Trembling, Corey banked the fire and blew out the lamp, then felt her way through the darkness to her own far corner of the room. Numbly she slipped out of her dress and put on her nightshift, said a swift, fervent little prayer, and crept between the cold sheets.

Another reminder of the distance between his world and hers—at home with Pa there had never been such a thing as a sheet. You wrapped yourself in a blanket and it was a whopping lot warmer. Corey thought, miserably, it would not hurt certain people to try it out.

Fourteen

Meg was shining like a sleek black filly as she hurried to catch up with Corey that sunny March afternoon a few days later. The only one of the family who had not lost some weight these past months, Meg seemed even to have filled out. Corey felt like a snapbean beside her.

"Are you bound for the store, Sister? I'll walk with you." She sounded dangerously sugary today. "My, it's been a month o' Sundays since I've seen you. I doubt you've even heard the news. Shad and I are betrothed."

"I wish you well," Corey said honestly.

"Not only that, but the Council has given us leave to wed at once, even before we reach the promised land. We can be sealed again properly when the new Temple gets built, but meanwhile the Church has granted us special permission to marry now, since

Shad's done such fine work this last year. I doubt if they'd do the same for you and Ethan, even if you were of age—which you aren't. Looks as if I'll be sitting near the head of the table before you, Sister."

The raillery didn't even prickle Corey. Right now she was just glad she was not sixteen yet, or the time of reckoning at hand. Ethan had been acting resentful of her ever since he'd got back from his trip. She'd never felt farther apart from him.

"I declare I can't imagine what your father saw in Ethan—" Meg was going on curtly when Corey cut in.

"It's not exactly fitting for you to make any remarks about my pa, seeing it's his army pay that's helped buy the goods in this store." Yanking open the door of the big log storehouse, she stalked inside ahead of Meg and went straight across to the counter to mingle with the other women. The large room was always crowded these days, what with everyone's supplies running low. The wives milled around the barrels and boxes of food-stuffs, hesitating between what they wanted and what they must have. Sometimes one would strike up a trade with another. But no one had an oversupply of tea.

Corey fingered the money Ethan had given her, thinking of the impatient way he had spoken this morning when she had told him they were nearly out. As he took a coin from his dwindling personal funds he said, "So be it. We must work for the community without pay, donate our extra food to the community poor, and yet when we run out of tea we must buy more—

from the community store. There's some reasoning about this that I don't care for."

Corey had been turning it over in her mind ever since, especially since it was Pa's own battalion pay that had helped to stock the store in the first place. It hardly seemed fair—as though one might be more fortunate to be penniless and receive free aid oneself. But surely there was no true virtue in that!

She tried to shove the doubts from her mind, and bent her thoughts on the small talk going on around her. The women seemed agog over something, their voices high with excitement.

". . . a stranger, you say?"

"Yes, with a piercing eye, almost as you'd picture an angel of the Lord. And the way he just appeared on my doorstep! He said he'd been summoned to heal us. Inspired by a vision from our martyred Prophet!"

This caused a ripple of awe.

"It's marvelous frightening," chimed in another. "He laid his hands on my head and prayed handsomely. Then he gave me some kind of healing water to drink —I guess it was holy water, it tasted beautiful, like green springtime. Right away I started to feel better."

"Your janders ain't all cleared up yet," another commented, eying her critically.

"I said I *feel* better," she insisted.

"Are you sure he's a real holy man? Has Brother Brigham told us to believe him?"

Another put in her word. "He says Brother Brigham

doesn't know him, because he's been in Missouri all these years since we left. He's had to stay there on a mission."

"What sort?"

"Likely it's a secret between him and the Prophet. Oh, he knew Joseph Smith—there's no doubt about that. He could quote him so fine—I swear, it took me back! I could almost hear the Prophet alive again and praying." Her eyes grew luminous with memory.

There were still some doubters. "How do you know for sure he's not some Missouri faker?"

"To come all the way here to pray over us? Why should he do that—asking no return? Fakers always scheme for money. I tell you this is a good man!"

Corey purchased a pound of tea and made her way back out of the crowd. A healer from Missouri—come so soon after Ethan had gone there? She couldn't dismiss it as coincidence. And when, upon reaching her own cabin, she heard voices coming from inside, the hunch grew stronger. Letting herself in, she paused uncertainly. A strange man was seated beside Sister Elizabeth's bed. The frail little lady was talking to him with a faint glow of her old liveliness.

"Corey, my dear, this is Mr. Seaton," she exclaimed. "He knew our Prophet intimately!"

The man stood up to bow to Corey—a wiry, balding little man with a ruddy face creased in smile wrinkles. But the look was almost as probing as the women had predicted. She nodded to him uneasily.

"I've heard. They say you were sent here by a vision."

"Not exactly, ma'am. The story may have been exaggerated in the telling," he answered tolerantly. "It was only a dream I had—there are all manner of dreams, you know."

"Yes, sir." She took off her cloak and hung it up, then went to Sister Elizabeth's side. "I'm sure you've been a great comfort to her, sir, but she's quite weak. I doubt if she should talk much longer."

"You're right, ma'am," he agreed readily. "I was just suggesting she'd better rest." And Sister Elizabeth did fade rapidly after any small outburst of excitement. Corey tucked her in, now, and she was almost asleep by the time the curtains were drawn. The stranger had moved over to stand by the hearth. Corey went to join him.

"As for me, sir, I have no ailments."

"I'm happy to hear it, ma'am." He studied her with a sudden shrewdness, though the pleasant look had warmed to open approval. "I hope you'll not mind my resting here a few moments longer—I have a wish to talk to young Ethan before I go. He should be along soon, shouldn't he?" Then, as if her private thoughts had echoed, Mr. Seaton went on, "The young man is responsible for my presence here. When he was in St. Joseph he came to me. It's the first I knew that the people up here were in such desperate need of a physician."

"And you—are?"

He nodded. "Ethan also mentioned that I could trust you, young lady. So I will. More than he bargained for. I will ask you a question that's been disturbing me: What misery is racking that boy's soul? Do you know?"

Corey stared at him resentfully. If she had, she'd not have told. "Excuse me, sir," she said warily, "but I must start the supper."

As she got out the makings of a stew, the little man watched moodily. "I can cure the ills of men's bellies and even their hearts, but the mind . . . the mind . . . Ethan's got some burden on his that will sicken him, as surely as if he were trying to carry an elephant on his back. If you could give me a clue I might prescribe for it."

Corey went on cutting up the vegetables, the salt pork. When she began to peel the potatoes the stranger walked over to the table, picked up a whole handful of the peelings, and dropped them into the stewpot. "Now," he said irritably, "you'll get nourishment, not just pulp." Then he went back to the fire to stand silent, hands locked behind him.

"Well, well," he muttered at last as if to himself, "you'll probably find it out at last—girls always do. Trouble is, will you have the sense to cope with it? Women tend to feed a man and forget him. Or beg for kisses. But I've a notion that boy needs more."

Then a silence settled on them broken only by the

soft clip of Corey's knife against the cutting board. From the corner of her eye she saw Mr. Seaton draw a big silver watch from his pocket. She herself was growing anxious, too. At last she went to glance out the door—it was growing dark outside. And then she saw Ethan coming, hurrying from the direction of town instead of from the prairie, as usual.

He came in quickly, breathing hard—made a swift motion of greeting to the man at the hearth and said to Corey, "Please—stay here at the door. If you see Dan coming, we've got to get Dr. Seaton out of here at once." Then going over to his guest he said, "I'm sorry to be late, sir. I was detained."

"Never mind, boy. Let's get to it." They sat down close together by the fire, while Corey took up a post near the door, holding it slightly ajar.

"Did you manage to see some of them?" Ethan was asking.

"Quite a few. It wasn't too difficult, since I actually did know the late Mr. Smith some years ago, and have a respect for his religion. If I took some slight liberties with the truth, I hope God—his and mine—will forgive me. The dreadful incidence of disease that I find here is enough to allay my conscience."

After that they went on in undertones—Corey caught only part of it.

". . . and what could be done for the biliousness?" Ethan asked intently.

". . . wintergreen . . . slight stimulant and diuretic

. . . cause of their digestive troubles is rotten food, for the most part. That will improve with the coming of spring . . ."

"Those sores on the children?"

". . . beginning signs of scurvy. They need apples . . ."

"There aren't many left."

"Then give them vinegar in water. It will help. Your worst problem . . . chest congestion, that high fever that takes them off. No real cure known . . . just give them tea, as much as they'll take. Try to make them sweat it out of their systems. Pile the blankets on . . ."

For an hour they spoke in the same guarded tones while Corey stared out into the darkness. It was full night outside when the physician finally stood up.

"I'd best be gone before Mr. Young discovers a Missourian in his camp."

"I wish they could know"—Ethan burst out impulsively—"I wish they could be told the risk you've taken to come here and help them. Maybe they wouldn't be so blind in their hatred."

"Son"—Dr. Seaton shook his head—"you didn't live through Missouri with the Mormons. They were slaughtered and ruined twice in five years. It'll take a long time to erase that memory. The day will come when they will accept a citizen from St. Joe in their midst—even a doctor. But meanwhile, don't rush them, my boy. And don't forget to pray with them, if you want to help. They've come this far on faith—don't underestimate it. It can work almost as many miracles as they think it can, though I still say a touch of vinegar helps." He shrugged into his coat and held out his hand. "Good luck, young man, and don't forget the matter I spoke of the other day."

When the door had closed behind him, Corey came to Ethan's side. He looked tired, not too well.

"There's a brave man," he said, "to ride so far, solely for the benefit of others. What a dedication to have—"

"You dared as much to go and bring him!" She laid a hand on his arm. But Ethan shook his head, as if failing some greater question.

Tentatively she asked, "What did he mean? What matter did he—?"

"A generous offer—to teach me. To let me work with him and learn. He didn't know what he was bargaining for. No, don't question me, Corey. I'm weary of questions. I spent a whole afternoon scrambling for answers."

"Dan?" she guessed anxiously.

He nodded. "And the whole Council of Apostles. Dan hauled me before the great men for judgment and sentencing. I knew it would come—he's been asking around about my activities ever since my absence from camp. But I thought he would deal with me himself."

"Did they judge you dreadful hard?"

"They were kinder than Dan. He wanted to drive the evil spirit out of me with a horsewhip. The Council was less emotional. They took a somewhat broader view of herbs and simples—even allowed that I meant well in trying to help the sick. What shocked them was the discovery that I'm—in their terms—a gentile. They didn't know they were harboring one in camp."

"They've not ordered you out!"

"They gave me a choice." Ethan shrugged. "To leave or to become one of them. I can see why. In a community such as this even one dissident voice could ruin a whole massive spirit of cooperation."

"And what did you—?" she began, but was afraid to finish the question or hear the answer—either answer.

"I told them," he said slowly, "that I am ready to become a Mormon. I'm to be baptized tomorrow."

Fifteen

Corey shivered. It had turned cold again overnight and a rough sky was racing low overhead as they stood on the riverbank that next afternoon. The whole family had gathered except for Lucy, who was still trying to get over her cough; she had volunteered to stay with Sister Elizabeth. But Millie's whole brood was there; they were dressed in their best clothes, even though the girls' hems were up to mid-shin and the boys' wrists hung long out of their sleeves. For all the winter had been severe they had shot up by inches. Trude was almost unchanged by the troublous months—just a trace more gaunt, and beneath the weathery skin her face had a winter pallor. Standing beside her Shad and Meg made a handsome pair. Corey felt a twinge as she glanced sidelong at Ethan. In contrast with Shad's lusty vigor he looked slender and haggard.

Dan clamped a massive hand upon his shoulder. "Bear up, son. You'll feel better once the Lord gets aholt on you."

The Elder who was going to officiate was a husky man, almost as big as Tanner. He stripped off his coat and Ethan followed suit, the chilly wind snapping his shirt sleeves, gusting the dark hair across his forehead as he stood bareheaded, waiting.

"You're certain you're ready to accept the faith, my son?" the Elder asked. "You truly seek remission of your sins?"

"Yes, sir," Ethan answered, though a buffet of wind nearly blew the words away.

"Then come." Taking the boy's arm, the Elder led him into the water, which was floating with chunks of muddy ice. On out deeper until it swirled around their waists. "I am commissioned by Jesus Christ to baptize thee. . . ." When he had finished, he put an arm behind Ethan's shoulders and ducked him under the water expertly.

"Do a good job, Elder!" Dan called from the bank. "All the way under!"

It seemed an awful endless moment that the old man held the boy down, then righted him again. Ethan shook the wet hair from his eyes and followed the Elder out of the river. Corey was waiting with his coat. He put it around his shoulders carelessly, carried his hat in hand as they all trooped back up toward the settlement.

Dan was in high spirits. "Now we're a family! No more angling and argument—we'll all be pulling on the same rope."

Walking beside Ethan, Corey was watching the water drip from his hair, wincing as she imagined how the cold air must cut through those wet clothes. But he seemed not to notice it. His eyes were half shut, almost as if he were saying some private prayer of his own. Once she thought his lips moved—she could even read the words: God forgive me.

Corey slept poorly that night—every little crackle of the banked fire seemed loud as a gun shot in the stillness of the cabin. Once she heard Sister Elizabeth moan in her sleep. And as morning drew on, the sound of Ethan's breathing, even from the far side of the room, seemed unnaturally hoarse.

As small noises began to be heard in the street outside, the stir of steps and muted greetings of early risers bound for work, Corey got up, glad that the night was over. Dressing quickly, she went to stir the fire, then bent over Ethan to waken him. He was hard asleep, the bedclothes in a tangle and half kicked aside. When she touched him, Corey was shocked at the burning warmth of his body—she could feel it through his nightshirt. Instinctively she laid a hand against his cheek. His skin was dry-hot.

Anxiously she tried to rouse him, but he only muttered and tossed. More frightened than ever, Corey shook him harder. At last he opened his eyes, but his look was unfocused and drowsy.

"Ethan, are you ill?" she demanded.

He mumbled something and lapsed back into a restless sleep.

"Corey, dear? What's the matter? Is something the matter?" Sister Elizabeth's voice came plaintively from the depths of her bed. Corey hurried over to quiet her.

"No, no. It's nothing—I'm sorry I spoke so loudly. Go back to sleep, Mother." The word usually soothed her—Sister Elizabeth sighed and nestled down in her pillows.

Corey went back to Ethan's side—she put her fingers on his wrist as she had watched him do so often, and in a moment felt the pump of his heart. Fast—much faster than her own. She was still crouching beside him, trying to think what to do, when she heard Dan's voice outside.

"Everybody risen in there?"

Hurrying to the door, Corey summoned him in. "I'm afraid Ethan's taken ill."

The big black-bearded man went across to hunker down at the boy's side. "It's the congestive fever," he said after a minute. "Hear that rattle in his breath? I've listened to that sound a-plenty this winter."

"He must have caught it from the baptizing," she murmured, frightened.

"Nonsense!" Dan told her sternly. "The Lord wouldn't bring fever on a man for such a reason. More likely there's still some devil at work in him—he's not had time to build up faith yet. Come here and pray with me." He took her hand, laying his other on Ethan's head and looking up in the direction of heaven. "We know this boy's erred some, Lord, but help him fight off the evil spirits that are lickin' through his body. Drive out the hellfire and bring him through. He'll make you a good man, I promise it! Fact is, I'll *see* to it! Amen." He straightened soberly. "That's all we can do, daughter. Keep watch beside him."

When she was alone again, Corey stood staring down at the man sprawled out limp on the mattress, and a fierce determination seized her. There must be something— It struck her that the earth floor must be cold. When she slipped a hand beneath the ticking, it felt clammy. Quickly she went to haul her own trundle bed from the corner—it wasn't too high off the ground but better than the floor. As she dragged it across the room, Sister Elizabeth called out again.

"Corey! Is something amiss?" There was a quaver in her voice. "Where's Ethan! I want to see him."

Going to her, Corey said gently, "Everything's all right—I was just moving a piece of furniture. Ethan isn't here now." But she could see the bewilderment coming on. "Wait, I'll bring you some tea." She closed the bed curtains, then hesitated, but only for a second. Reaching up, she opened the secret compartment and took out one packet. As she stirred the contents into a cup of tea she offered a mute apology to some all-seeing presence that seemed to be with her in the silent room.

I'm sorry if it's wrong—I'm sorry. I don't know what else to do. I can't stay with her today—not and tend to Ethan, too. I've got to help him. Somehow.

The hours that followed were like a bad dream—not too real. Summoning all her strength, Corey managed to get Ethan into her own bed, which she had set close to the fire. But he was hard to manage, struggling against her efforts to care for him, throwing aside the quilts she heaped on him, talking incoherently in an undertone. Once she heard the word "father."

As she bent over him he seemed not to know her at all and twisted away from the tea she set to his lips. It was all she knew to do—tea and warm blankets, the doctor had said. Bring out a sweat. There were times when Ethan's forehead was damp, but the fever kept on mounting.

That night she dragged his mattress over next to the bed and lay down on it without changing to her night clothes. She didn't get much rest—it was a constant task to keep him covered. But toward morning she must have fallen asleep out of pure exhaustion, for when she wakened the room was cold, the fire low. Ethan lay still at last, and that frightened her worse than his tossing.

Turning up the lantern, she made a new blaze on the hearth and came back to his side. He was much worse—she knew it without knowing how. The fever was still raging. Through parched lips he drew each breath with such difficulty she was afraid there wouldn't be another. As she stared down at him, panic-stricken, Dan tapped and came in.

For a long moment he stood looking at the boy, his swarthy face knit with concern. At last he got down on his knees beside the bed and began to pray silently—the only time Corey had ever seen him do such a thing. It almost gave her hope for some stroke of instant heavenly healing. But Ethan didn't stir. When he rose to go, Dan faced her bleakly.

"Do you want me to send Trude or Millie to help you?"

Corey shook her head. "I can care for him." Because now she was beginning to sense what she must do—or try to do. As soon as Dan was gone, she went to the locked chest. All day yesterday it had been a silent temptation, sitting there with its mysterious contents, and she, not able to tell whether they were good or evil. Searching through Ethan's pockets, she found the key and unlocked the box. Her hands were none too steady as she picked up the bottles, looking for familiar labels. Camphor. Eucalyptus. Mustard Seed. She took the stoppers out and sniffed them—the camphor had a nose-tingling smell.

Taking it back to the bed, she held it near Ethan's face. After a while he stirred slightly, enough so that she was able to get a little tea down him, though he never really roused from that terrible stupor. And having ventured so far, she felt a powerful impulse to go on.

Working quickly, she prepared a paste of meal, just as he had, though when it came to adding drops of these medicaments a surge of anxiety came over her. She supposed they could be harmful if they weren't used right. Cautiously she added a drop, then another. Finally, when the mixture began to raise aromatic fumes, she tried a little on her wrist. It seemed harmless enough. Spreading it on a cloth, she took it over to the bed, opened Ethan's nightshirt, and placed the poultice on his chest. Tensely she sat by his side, holding his hand beneath the blankets, trying to sense any smallest change in him, for better or worse.

Time seemed to stand still. Only when Sister Elizabeth stirred did she leave him for a moment. Or when the fire burned low. A cold wind was still whipping around the cabin, fingering to find any slight crack where the chinking had fallen from the logs. The sound of it made a mournful frame for the stillness of the room.

At last Ethan moved, making a vague, fretful effort to pluck at the poultice. Lifting a corner of it, Corey saw that his chest was red, and small blisters were forming. Frantically she took the application off, blaming herself bitterly for daring to try such a thing. And yet he seemed nearer the surface than he had been. She made another cup of tea and tried once more to get it down him. Without opening his eyes, he swallowed some of it, and a heavy sweat broke out almost at once. It streamed down his cheeks—his hair was as wet as when he'd come from the river.

Hurriedly she dried his face, but the nightshirt was soaked, too. It was no time for self-consciousness—she threw the covers aside and undressed him. His body was gleaming with sweat. Toweling him dry, she wrapped a blanket around him and covered him with the quilts again, made a fresh pot of tea. Again and again in those next hours the perspiration started out. He was taking the tea a little better now, as she held him propped against her shoulder.

"Come, Ethan, please—a little more—" She whispered it a hundred times, and again a hundred.

By late afternoon she had used the last dry blanket she had. The tea was almost gone. When she brewed it this time she summoned her daring again and added a few drops of wintergreen, remembering the doctor had called it a stimulant. When she raised Ethan in the curve of her arm, Corey thought he looked less flushed. She laid her cheek against his brow—it was cooler. For an instant she held him in a tight, thankful embrace. Then—the tea again.

This time, as she let him lie back against the pillow, he opened his eyes to look up at her wearily. He seemed dazed, but his vision was clear. Corey tried to smile at him as if nothing much was wrong—the way he always did, to reassure a patient. She could understand so much more about Ethan now—and something else. About herself. Love might be a foolish conceit with some girls, but for her it was like the turn of a knife in her heart.

Sixteen

For months the leather trunk had stood unopened in Corey's corner of the room. Now she lifted the lid and took out the pair of trousers and hunting shirt she used to wear—it seemed a hundred years ago. Nervously she skinned out of her dress and began to put on the old clothes. Though she was screened by the curtained bedstead, she was still acutely conscious of the fact that Ethan was just beyond. With a comforter around his shoulders and a blanket across his knees he was propped up in a chair by the fire.

He had been slow to mend, these two weeks since the fever had left him. For all he tried to rally his strength—and Corey had never seen anyone strive more intently—he still was so weak he had to hold onto her to walk from the bed to a seat before the hearth. The worst of it was that he couldn't force himself to eat much. And for good reason—the smell of the salt pork was enough to turn a well man's stomach, rancid as it was after all these months. And it was the only meat they had. The Council had long since ruled that only families without any food at all could take an occasional animal from the herd.

Corey tucked in her shirttail and buckled the belt. The shirt was tighter than it had been a few months ago—she felt a reluctance to go before him in this garb, but reminded herself that it didn't matter much. Ethan would never consider her a delicate sort, so he might as well be completely disenchanted and think her outright brazen. And yet when she pulled on the scuffed old boots it made her wince to realize how crude they would seem to him. Quickly she braided her hair, which fell below her shoulders now, and pinned it around the crown of her head. Then, bracing herself, she went around to the fireplace.

Ethan looked up wonderingly.

"I'm going hunting," she told him. "We could all use some fresh meat. I'd like to borrow your coat and pistol."

It was difficult to read his look—his eyes seemed more deep-set than ever since his illness and the faint smile could have meant anything. "I've sometimes tried to imagine how you looked before you came to us," he mused. Then added, "Take anything of mine you need."

"Before I go, let me help you back to bed."

He made a little gesture of compliance. "It's a poor

patient who argues with his nurse." Laying aside the quilt, he let her help him up, his arm around her shoulders. If one good thing had come from all this, it was their closeness to each other. The shyness was gone. He no longer started away from her when she touched him, or blushed when she showed him some kindness. Now, he sank onto the bed as if his knees were loose.

"Don't suppose," he said, with fleeting humor, "that I'm unaware of who is most in need of this meat you're going after. I'm grateful, Corey."

Flustered, she smoothed his pillow and covered him with the quilt, then went to take down his coat. The pistol was in one pocket, together with a pouch of powder and shot.

"The gun has a slight cast to the right," he said. "About an inch at thirty feet."

She buttoned on the coat—it was too large, of course, but with the knapsack strapped across it she didn't feel clumsy. In fact, she felt more herself than she had in months. And yet she wished she could truly interpret his smile as he said, "Good hunting."

It was a relief to get out of the cabin for a while. The closeness of the sickroom and the confinement of her own feelings had constricted her until she was nearly rigid inside. Now she drank in the cold March air and stretched into a long stride. As she walked down through the thin sunshine she fingered the loaded gun in her pocket.

Along the river's edge below town trees clustered and there was a good stand of brush. She felt fairly sure the backwash of the river would harbor some sort of water-fowl—whole flights of them had been going north. Nearly every night she heard the high, ragged cry of geese overhead.

Once she was in the dense growth she slowed down and moved stealthily, listening for the mutter of conversation that would betray a flock upon the water. The wind was blowing toward her, which gave her some advantage. Wet ground softened her steps—snow still lay beneath the bushes. And then she froze in her tracks as a low line of ducks appeared, skimming the willow tops, heading her way. While she held her breath they spread wing and put down just ahead. She could hear them plainly. With all the caution she had learned from Pa, Corey crept forward a step at a time.

Through a break in the willows she saw them at last, paddling, turning end-up to feed in the swampy margin of the little inlet. She was ankle-deep in water, every step taking her deeper now and risking the fright of the whole flock. It would be hard to get one on the wing with a strange gun. She decided to risk a long shot.

Carefully she sighted along the barrel of the pistol; it was heavier than Pa's old Black Hawk. She knew she should have tried it first to get the feel of it, but powder was so dear. . . . She drew bead on the nearest drake, adjusted the aim, as Ethan had advised, and squeezed the trigger. The roar of the gun mingled with the rush of wings—she felt a pounding elation, for the duck lay dead.

She splashed forward to pick it up, but the water

deepened sharply and she was up to her knees before she knew it.

"Hold on, ma'am. I'll retrieve for you." It was a man on horseback who had just ridden up through the woods. Giving heels to his stout roan, he rode out to where the bird floated and scooped it up.

"I'm grateful, sir." She smiled as he reined up beside her and handed the bird down. "I reckon I'd have had a soaking."

"You must want that fowl fairly bad." He looked her over curiously. A stocky man, of forty years or so, with clean-shaven face and farmerish clothes; his quizzical look reminded her of Pa. "Are you from the encampment yonder, ma'am?" he asked.

"Yes, sir." Corey sat down on a nearby log and began to clean the duck.

"I'm glad to hear it. I've been told that the Saints tend to subdue their wives. You give me hope that the rumor is unfounded."

Corey glanced at him warily. "You talk as if you're not one of us."

"Yes. Oh, yes, I am." And yet she had the feeling he was not quite telling all the truth. When he got down off his horse, she was certain there was no stone caught in its shoe as he was pretending. "Have I had the pleasure to see you at prayer meeting—in some other, less distinctive clothing?"

"I've not been to many since we came," she confessed. "Too many ill folks to attend."

"It puts a trial upon us all," he agreed gravely. "I must say that some seem to meet it with more imagination than others. I have to admire the person who relies upon his own resources, as you have with this duck, instead of expecting heaven to solve all things at the drop of a prayer."

"I reckon I was praying when I pulled the trigger," she informed him dryly. There was something odd about this talk—she knew he was trying to draw her out for some reason. "Truth is," she added, "my man's been ill near to death. He needs this meat."

"Perhaps you'll flatter my curiosity on one matter: what view does he take toward the practicality of your costume?"

"He's not said," she replied cautiously. "But my pa—Judd Tremaine—he raised me this way. And he's a good man, so it must be all right. Anyway, you can't hunt birds in a skirt."

"Tremaine—I don't believe I know a Tremaine."

"He's not with us—he's in the Battalion. I'm traveling with Dan Tanner's household. If he was to see me this way he'd skin me, likely."

"Ah, yes, I know Brother Tanner. A good man, and industrious." His interest slanted off in another direction. "I'd not have supposed one of his family would be reduced to such narrow straits for want of food."

"We have food, such as I can eat, but the wheat's full of weevils and the lard stinks. It turns a sick man's stomach. Dan says we must save every cent we've got to buy provisions come next summer when we head west, and the Council won't let us kill off any more of our beef. I wonder—" She broke off as a strange whimsy struck her. Then as she saw the stranger was waiting for her to go on, she said, "I was just wondering; when we get to Zion, you reckon the Council will take a duck like this away from me and sell it in the store?"

The man looked genuinely shocked. "I should hope not."

"That's what they're doing right now—taking my pa's battalion pay and buying food to sell in the store and I've no money to buy it."

He rubbed his chin thoughtfully. "That is a rather distressing twist. But then if the food were given without charge, there'd be no money to buy more for the great venture ahead of us. You do agree that it's worth some sacrifice—to face such a magnificent prospect? A new city to build—earth that's never been turned before. A garden to bring forth out of a desert somewhere so remote that no one but ourselves will ever govern it. What a goal!"

"It seems a long way off," she said, stowing the duck in her knapsack.

"But nearer than before. I'm an old farmer—I can smell the sap rising, and these wet clods mean green grass. I'd say spring is near upon us. A beautiful day"—he swung up onto his horse—"a fine day to be on the move."

As he went his way and she walked on along a path

through the woods, Corey wondered why she felt provoked—oddly excited. There was no reason, nothing important about it ever to remember again. And yet the look of the stranger's face had somehow made her relish the day and she, too, could scent the turn of the season. For the first time in a long while Corey thought of the adventure ahead of them all, and her heart began to beat faster.

It was nearly dark when she reached the cabin—light showed in a thin crack beneath the door. She supposed Lucy was there; she'd promised to look in on the invalids while Corey was away. But when she let herself in, she was stopped short by the sight of the whole family arrayed around the room.

Dan commanded the hearth, feet spread, hands on hips. Trude and her daughters and Millie were grouped around Sister Elizabeth, who sat up in bed, obviously fluttered by all the attention. Ethan was still stretched out in the trundle bed, while Shad leaned against the footboard lazily. As he took in Corey's clothes, a slow grin spread across his face. She felt her cheeks flame—everyone was staring at her. The women looked instantly scandalized and Dan's face was forbidding.

"So here y'are, daughter. We feared you had come to harm."

"Game's scarce, sir." As steadily as she could, she walked forward and brought out of her knapsack the roll of oilcloth in which she'd wrapped the game. Laying the duck and a pair of quail on the table, she said,

"I'm sorry if you were worried."

"What indecent trappings do you call those?" Dan made a short motion that included the breeches and coat.

Corey felt her dander rise. "My pa didn't think they were indecent. He might have thought it more so for the menfolk of a family to leave the hunting to a woman."

"And who said ye had to go a-hunting?"

"Common sense," she retorted. "Spoiled food is no provision to bring a man back to health. And you'll be wanting to work Ethan, like enough, when we take the trail!"

In the ringing silence Sister Elizabeth spoke up stanchly. "Dan, I think she looks charming! Like Diana, the huntress."

And even if Diana was some old Greek goddess, Corey could have kissed the little Englishwoman.

Shad remarked insinuatingly, "What I want to know —what was she doing when she wasn't plugging birds?"

"That's a foolish question." Corey was still seething with defiance.

"Not so," Dan said sourly. "I want to know it, too. What have you been up to, daughter?"

"Up to? Up to my knees in the river."

"Who did you meet on this expedition?"

"No one." Then she corrected herself. "Except one man on horseback who brought me the duck from deep water."

"What else passed between you? What did you tell him?"

"Nothing. I mean, we talked of the day, the weather—of the journey west. He spoke wonderfully of the promised land."

"I'll warrant." Dan gave an uneasy laugh. "And you spoke of us—this family. You told him we were poor, short of food, and stingy with money?"

"No such! I may have said our stock of goods was low, as everyone else's." She looked around at them, puzzled. "Why do you ask me all this?"

"Because you've received a gift." Dan pointed to a box that had escaped her notice up to now, half hidden beyond the table. A wicker hamper, it was full of food—meal and flour and jellies, even dried fruits. She stared down at it amazed.

"It came to our cabin first," Dan told her. "With this."

Corey took the card from him. On one side was written: "To Miss Tremaine of Tanner's House." And on the reverse were the words, "The Lord helpeth the man who helps himself." It was signed "Brigham Young."

When they had all gone home at last Corey tried to slip back into her usual demeanor, changed to her dress, fixed the supper, and helped Sister Elizabeth prepare for the night. But she was conscious of a reckoning yet to come between her and Ethan. All through the talk he had stayed quiet, but when they were alone together at last, the room was charged with unspoken emotion.

Clearing away the dishes, she prepared to face him with fierce, proud phrases. It had been a rare occasion to meet such a man as their leader. She wasn't ashamed of the way she had talked up to him. Or of the meat she'd brought back. After all, Ethan had eaten that duck with more appetite than he'd shown in months. When she finished the chores, she came deliberately to stand before him on the hearthstone. Once more he was sitting up, on the couch before the fire.

"The supper," he said slowly, "was wonderful. I know how much effort it cost you to get it. I don't know why you should have done this—for me."

It was so much the opposite of what Corey had expected that her defiance crumbled. "I'm sorry!" she said in a rush. "I'm sorry to have shamed you in front of them all. If I'd known they were here—"

"Corey!" he broke in, on a keen note of shock. "What are you saying?"

"I know I looked disgraceful."

"You looked—you looked—" He hesitated, then burst out, "I was never so proud in my life!"

Tears sprang to her eyes and spilled down her cheeks. "Proud of *me?*"

Ethan started to struggle to his feet—when she made him sit back he caught her hands and drew her down beside him on the couch. Awkwardly he put his arms around her. "Please don't cry. What did I say?"

"I always thought you detested my—my bold ways."

He drew her closer with a quick regret, as if she had hurt him. "I know I'm not good at speaking out what I feel, but it never occurred to me you thought I scorned you in any way. Good Lord, Corey, I love you!"

Wordlessly she looked up through her tears and tried to comprehend what he had said.

"Why shouldn't I?" he went on more gently. "You're wonderful. The way you speak out, when you believe in a thing. The way you take hold of the rough edges of life. You're so able—of all things I value that. What you do, you do well. Ever since the day you split Shad's log for him I've—I've—"

"I thought that made you angry."

"I was upset, because I knew then what was happening to me and it was more than I'd bargained for."

"But why did you agree to the betrothal, if you didn't expect to—?" Corey took a sudden guess. "For your mother's sake?"

"I did think," he admitted, "that it would be good for her to have another woman with her. But mainly I did it because I thought it a hard lot for a girl to be bound to some man who would wed her without love. I was trying to win you a little time to cast about for a man who would truly cherish you. The one thing I didn't reckon on was that I might come to love you myself. I tried not to let it happen, but that was futile. Then I tried not to let you know—"

"But I feel the same way!" she protested fervently.

"I've suspected as much. That's why lately I've tried to put you off from me. But I couldn't let you think I somehow held you in contempt. Not that. So now—it's all told." He rubbed at his eyes miserably. "What a trick for fate to play on us, Corey."

The hopelessness of his tone dismayed her. "Why do you say that!"

"For so many reasons. How could we ever be married? Even if I had something to offer—a future or a plan for the future—but I don't. I'm walking on a thin crust from day to day. Could I ask a girl to share such a wretched existence? No, don't stop me—you don't know how deep it goes. Everything I once wanted to do and be has turned hollow in me."

"But there's always a new start—"

"Even if I thought so, there's an even greater barrier. Corey—I'm no Mormon. I can lie to Dan or the Council, even to my mother, but I can't lie to you. I can't change my faith, either. I have my own religion—it was my father's. It's founded on tolerance, among other things. I can't accept the notion that only the Mormons will reach heaven—that the Lord has guaranteed them some higher place than other good men, such as Dr. Seaton, who is a gentile. But"—his arm fell from around her—"I have no right to change you or alter your beliefs. Today you were beautiful—looking ahead. It fired you up to talk with Brigham Young, and I can understand why. He's a man who knows where he's going. A great man. Nothing is going to stand in his way. I'm sure he will bring the Church through to some far place where its curious doctrines will bear fruit. I almost envy you—I wish I could follow him without question, but I can't. And what's worse, I have nothing better to offer." He looked at her helplessly. "When the time comes that I turn aside from this trek, you mustn't try to follow me. Because for me there is no promised land."

PART THREE

Seventeen

In the vast, endless, rippling prairie land the column of wagons wound slowly westward, crawling over the rise and fall of the land. A thin thread of life under the hot June sun. White canvas gave off a blinding glare; the river glittered like a sheet of brown glass, this shallow, muddy Platte, all tangled in its willows and islands.

Hot, hard going. The dust made a grit in the mouth. But as the land began to steepen and the oxen leaned into the yoke, Corey felt the rise of a pulsing excitement. Ethan, too, could hardly keep his eyes off the horizon that rose around them like the rim of a giant dish.

Once he'd said wonderingly, "I think all England could lie here in the bottom of this saucer."

Even Corey, raised in a trackless forest, hadn't been prepared for these long stretches of grassland. It was the thickest, tallest grass she'd ever seen, high as a buffalo's shoulders. There were times when they came upon the monstrous beasts before they knew it, and a whole herd would thunder off, spreading across the land in a tide of brown fur.

For all its quiet, it was a frightening land. Overhead big hawks wheeled watchfully, and from underfoot rattlers slithered for their holes. Even more ominous to some was the stir of dust that rose across the river on the south bank, where the gentiles' wagon trains followed their "Oregon trail," as they called it. It caused anxious muttering among the fearful—grim talk of Missourians and mobs, but that seemed groundless to Corey. It was easy to see that those folk over there were having their own trials. The disjointed little groups scattered and re-formed and bunched and straggled. A poor showing compared to the orderly procession of Saints.

Before Brigham Young had left with a small advance party, to search out the unmapped land ahead, he had organized the first wave of the migration to be carried out. While some families were to stay back in Winter Quarters and grow crops, others were instructed to take the trail as soon as warm weather permitted, and Dan Tanner's family was among the fortunate chosen to go. Altogether three thousand would head westward, group by group, during the summer, but there was no crowding or lagging. The multitude was divided into parties of "tens"—ten families traveling as a unit, governed by a captain who had been appointed by the Council. Because of Tanner's skills he and his wagons had been assigned to one of the earliest groups to leave. And now as Corey scanned the vast country behind them, the trail of well-disciplined trains followed along so evenly spaced, she wondered if even Ethan couldn't see some worth in the way the migration was moving.

As she walked beside him one day, helping keep the oxen stepping along, she risked a mention of it. They had topped a slight rise from which they could look across to the uneven line of wagons on the far side of the river.

"We're making better time than those," she said. "See that one with the top painted red? Far back down there? It was ahead of us two days ago."

"Maybe the man stopped to hunt," Ethan said shortly. It was irritating him that the Council had given orders no one was to be allowed to spend powder and shot for game except certain appointed marksmen.

"More likely they're arguing over who should be captain," Corey remarked. "I've heard they spend a mortal lot of time changing leaders."

"My congratulations to them! I wish we had that privilege. If it slowed us up, at least we'd feel like freer men when we did move on."

Corey felt a flutter of agitation, sensing some truth in the pent-up declaration, yet torn by all her teaching from Pa and the others. "But our captain is an Elder. He's become that because he's wise."

"He's also human, just as I am, and can be mistaken. No one can know everything that lies ahead." His face was flushed with vision and wishfulness such as Corey had never seen there before.

It came to her how Ethan had changed these weeks since they had taken the trail west. The inward brooding had given way to restlessness. He had never again spoken to her of love, but it was in his eyes when they were alone together. She wondered, now, if it was this which made him glance out around him with that searching look.

She was startled out of her musing by the sight of a small figure up ahead. Sammy, pounding back along the trail. As he came up, there was a wide-eyed urgency in his face.

"Mama just fell down," he panted in an ecstasy of fright. "She's all lying there and nobody to drive the oxen and Sarah's crying and—"

Corey and Ethan exchanged glances quickly. He had told her weeks ago he suspected Millie was in a family way. Now she saw the impulse come over him to go to her assistance—then he shook his head.

"You go. Dan's been keeping an eye on me," he said. "It's probably just vertigo. Make her lie down awhile. Call me if you really need me."

Corey picked up her skirts and followed Sammy back up the trail. As she reached the wagon, Sarah and Samantha were helping their mother inside. She was pale but smiling.

"I'm sorry if Sammy startled you," she called to Corey. "I just felt a touch of heat. I'll be all right in a minute."

"Rest awhile," Corey told her. "I'll drive your team. Sarah, you stay with her—put a damp cloth on her forehead." As she took up the whip, Sammy fell in step with her, swinging an empty basket with nervous energy.

"Mama's going to have a baby," he announced.

Ten-year-old Samantha had jumped back down out of the wagon in time to hear. "He's not supposed to know that!" she gasped. "You've been eavesdropping, you awful little monkey."

"I don't care," he yelled. "Pretty soon I won't be second littlest any more, I'll be *third* littlest, and I'll get bigger than you and I'll punch you." He made a menacing gesture.

Corey got between them. "If that basket isn't full of buffalo chips by suppertime you'll catch a licking," she told him. "And you, Samantha, aren't you supposed to be watching the churn?" The jolting wagon churned the milk of its own motion, but the butter had to be skimmed off every so often.

Samantha shook her head, the sunbonnet flouncing. "Sarah can do it while she sits with Mama."

"Is Mama going to have the baby right now?" Sammy asked hopefully.

"You git!" Samantha slapped his backside. "Quick, or I'll tell the Elder you're sinful lazy."

"I hate buffaloes," he said glumly. "They stink." But

he scuffed off into the brush where the other children were roaming in search of the dried buffalo dung which was the only fuel to be had in this treeless land. Samantha walked on beside Corey, whirling in circles, to make her skirts flare.

"Meg's going to have a baby, too. And so is the brindle cow, did you know? And the Webers' dear little goat has two of the prettiest lambs. Don't you wish you could, too? I do!"

"Goats don't have lambs," Corey said absently. The secret truth was that as the spring-born young had begun to trot at the heels of the herd, she had felt a nameless yearning warmth for the little things, and her loneliness had deepened. Samantha was watching her curiously.

"Do you like Ethan?"

"Yes," Corey said softly.

"Why?"

"What a question!"

"Well, I don't. Or anyhow, I didn't. He told Mama to make us drink vinegar water, it's awfully nasty. But then he was nice the other day when the bee stung me—he put saleratus on it and it quit hurting. I guess he's smart. But why does he always want to dig all the time?"

A lot of people had been puzzled when, that first day the chores were assigned, Ethan had insisted stubbornly that he be given all the spadework as his share of the common duty.

"You'd think he would have got his bellyful of it this winter," Dan had grumbled. "I'd just as leave not see one of my family digging the sumps for this whole shebang of people."

For once Sister Trude had stood up to her husband. "He's the kind of man who's got to be good at a thing, to do it willing. He's learned to be handy with a shovel. And even a slop pit's better if it's dug neat. There's worse things than being a stickler." And that closed the discussion.

Now Corey looked at Samantha and said whimsically, "You can dig a hole and still think about other things. Ethan's always thinking."

"I thought something once," the little girl said idly, "I thought real hard and I thought I didn't want to be somebody's second wife, like Mama. It made Papa awfully mad—he prayed over me good."

For all that it was childish prattle it disturbed Corey unnaturally. Now that she knew the keen pang of love herself, she felt an overwhelming distaste for the whole thought of sharing a man with other women. And yet, it was said to be sinful even to let such a thought come to mind.

After supper chores were over that evening she sat down on the back steps of the wagon and looked out toward the flickering lights that were beginning to prick the dusk along the far side of the river. In a little while Ethan came out and, without a word, sat down beside her. He was the only person, beside Pa, that she could sit quiet with and not feel uneasy.

It was growing cool. Far out across the prairies a coyote yelped and another answered with a long, rising wail. Corey shivered, and Ethan put an arm around her lightly.

"Don't tell me there's something you're afraid of?"

"It's a lonesome sound."

"And fit for this country. I wish my father could have seen this," he went on distantly. "He always wanted to come, but never would desert the patients who depended on him. I think if he had seen how rough a land this is, how far apart the settlements will be, and how great the need for physicians, he might have broken away and come. But he'd have been traveling over there." He looked across at the distant watch fires of the gentile camps. "So would I, but for Mother. . . ." His face knit with concern as he glanced over his shoulder at the silent wagon. It was smaller than the old one, sturdier built, but there had been no room for the bedstead and other furniture, the tapestries and figurines. Though they had made her bunk as comfortable as possible, Sister Elizabeth had shrunken down into her pillows and stayed very quiet these days.

At the sorrow in his face Corey forgot the argument, forgot everything except the unspoken thought that was grieving him. "They say the western climate is healthful. I know she'll get better as soon as we reach Zion."

Almost remotely he said, "My mother has an ailment

of the blood. It's been coming on gradually for years. Father was working to find a cure for it when he died. She's been weakening steadily ever since, and Dr. Seaton last spring confirmed it. He said she couldn't last another six months."

Shock and dismay made a confusion inside Corey. This whole long while he had lived with that terrible knowledge—and then the fact itself bore in on her with a sharp stab of grief. In the dusk she stared up at him, brimming with words she didn't know how to speak.

Ethan held her a little closer. "Don't be afraid, Corey. My father always said that to die is natural—nothing to be afraid of. He believed in a better life to come, if a man had earned it—if a man keeps faith with himself. In her own way, my mother's always done that. Sometimes I almost envy her, because—for her—the worst is nearly over."

Eighteen

It seemed little short of a miracle to find a whole lively settlement of people sprung up in the middle of nowhere. Corey had heard of Fort Laramie, at the crossroads where the north-and-south route from Santa Fe met the Oregon trail. But she had pictured it as some desperate little outpost fortified against the Indians. Instead, it was a gay, teeming market place where the Indians were as welcome as anyone else.

It was well stocked with supplies fresh out of Independence, but the prices were outrageous. With flour $1.00 a pound, Corey was glad they had been able to purchase their own goods back in Winter Quarters, for just the cost of bringing the goods to the store there. However, she enjoyed watching the other shoppers—people of all descriptions, rubbing elbows in the big courtyard within the square walls of the Fort. Even more lolled in the shade outside—Santa Fe traders and mountain men and migrators, freckled farm girls and bullwhackers, all thronged together in a momentary fellowship in this solitary meeting place, the only one in two thousand miles of wilderness.

Even the Mormons were drawn into a cautious mingling. Out here, where the big emotion was the drive westward, the coming of their train had stirred little excitement. And so, as the "tens" had come up, group by group, their captains had ordered a stopover, just as the gentile trains were doing. With good forage for the stock, it was an ideal place to rest up for the long, dangerous pull ahead. The mountains were all around them now, harsh rugged chains of hills, rising into farther, colder heights.

But for these few brief days the Saints put their worries aside. They ventured shyly into the Fort. Of an evening a few even dared to join the gentiles' dances, which turned out to be not so very different from their own.

With this respite from the rock and sway of the wagon, Sister Elizabeth seemed to revive slightly. She had hardly eaten along the way, only forcing down a few bites at Ethan's gentle insistence. Now, sitting propped against her pillows one morning, she remarked weakly that she was a trifle hungry.

"I believe I could eat a bit of fresh meat," she added.

Ethan hesitated. The hunting detachments were instructed to seek out only buffalo and deer, so as to feed as many people as possible from each kill. And though

Dan had managed to secure some of the more tender parts for Sister Elizabeth, the meat was too wild and strong-flavored for her delicate taste.

"Of course if there isn't any—" she faltered.

"We'll get you some." Ethan smiled at her confidently. "I think I know where I can discover a choice supper, if you can spare me for the day. And Corey, too. I'll need her along. We can ask Lucy to come over and keep you company."

"Delightful!" Sister Elizabeth said, with a touch of her old gaiety.

It was easily enough arranged, but Corey was mystified as she set off with Ethan. The day was beautiful—warm, but not with the green summer heat of the Mississippi bottoms that she had always known. This air was clear and dry and incredibly fresh. The breeze down off the mountain slopes smelled of flowers. Ethan, too, kept looking off toward that high country, but his face was troubled.

"There's the pull that will tax Mother's strength. The altitude makes the air thinner, the heart works harder."

Corey didn't understand it completely, but she sensed what he meant. Even here, she had to breathe faster, and when she hurried a slight dizziness came over her.

"That's why we must do everything possible to build her up." He stooped to pick a bird's feather out of the grass, the coral wing feather of a flicker. "Come on, I'll show you a trick I'll wager you never saw done back in Iowa."

They had been following the little brook that flowed down behind the Fort, climbing higher as they went, up into a valley of the foothills. It was a pleasant stream, clear as crystal. Now he paused beside it speculatively while she sat down on a broad, flat rock, just glad for the warmth of the sun on her back and his nearness.

"Let me see—it's been a while since I did this." He took a spool of red thread from his pocket. "I borrowed that from your sewing box." Then he took out a fish-hook which he began to wind with thread. Stripping a small section from the feather, he tied it to the hook. "So much for the tail. Now we need hackle." He lifted the tip of one of Corey's braids which she had let fall loose over her shoulders. "Beautiful as a badger's fur. May I have a snip?"

"As much as you like," she told him humorously. "I always did prefer it short."

"There we disagree slightly." He let his hand rest an instant against the curve of her neck. "I like those long locks." Then, carefully, he cut a few strands of hair and tied them onto the hook. "I believe we should have a wing."

"I wish you'd tell me what you're doing."

But Ethan was searching in the reeds along the bank of the stream. He seemed to find what he wanted and brought it back—the brown spotted feather from a duck's breast. Tying that on toward the eye of the hook, he knotted the thread expertly. "An ancient formula for the catching of trout. One of my countrymen set down the directions in a book—which may seem a curious source for baiting a hook, but it serves well. At least my father and I had good luck with artificial flies in the brooks in England."

"These are American fish." She laughed. "They may not be fooled by your British shenanigans."

"We'll see. I'll make you one, too, and I vow you'll be converted to this sport." As he tied a second fly he went on more soberly. "I don't know that the stream will have fish, but I've seen a few rise in the Platte, and this water looks even better. Now to cut some willows with enough whip to cast well."

When he had rigged the makeshift poles with fish-line and attached a fly to the end of each, he gave her one. "You start downstream. I'll go above and fish down until I reach you. The knack of it is to keep moving. If a fish doesn't strike at your first cast, draw the line back and try again, each time just below the last. And be quiet, of course—but then I needn't tell you that. You probably know the ways of fish better than I do."

With a certain pride, Corey thought that she did know something about them. She'd grown up with a pole in her hand. Now, looking at the stream, she could imagine a trout lying beneath the far bank where the swift current made a back eddy. Softly she moved down the shore and whipped the willow pole to send the line shooting forth into the riffle. Nothing happened except that her hook fouled itself on a rock. With a yank, she pulled it free—it flew back straight for her face. Throwing out a hand, she warded off the backlash, though the hook stung her palm sharply.

More intently she tried again, and saw it was going to take practice to make that hook behave like a real insect on the water. After half an hour she was doing better—at least she thought so, and had even seen the swirl of a fish from time to time near the fly; once a small one jumped clear out of the water after it. Sometimes she felt them snatch at it, but never managed to seat the hook. After another hour of trying she began to face the sorry truth—that there was some secret to this sport she had not guessed.

She had come within sight of the Fort again now, and sat down on a log to wait for Ethan. She was in no hurry to go back to that hurry and scurry, though fortunately the sounds of it didn't reach this far. It was wonderfully still around her; the hum of bees and the skip of the brook just made the silence seem more comfortable. The log was warm from the sun; all around it grew clumps of wild strawberry. Idly Corey leaned forward and spread the leaves to discover a cluster of berries beneath, full-ripe. Going down on her knees, she began to pick them, putting them in a half-round of bark that she pried loose from the log.

She was lost in her work when a footstep made her glance up, to find Ethan paused on the bank, watching her as if he were trying to memorize the picture of her there. Corey smiled at him as he came over.

"I haven't any fish to boast of, so I thought to earn

my keep one way or another."

He bent and tasted one of the berries with appreciation. "Mother will be overwhelmed. She loves them. But I don't understand—you made no catch at all?"

"No. Did you?"

He unslung his knapsack and opened it to show her half a dozen silver beauties bedded in fresh grass. "The stream is alive with them. I kept more than we need—I thought to give some to Lucy and Sister Trude."

The sight of them wakened an old hunger. Corey shook her head. "I just don't have the knack, but I'll try to make up for it in the cooking."

Ethan had picked up the rod which she had laid aside. Looking at the fly, he exclaimed, "No wonder! Somewhere you must have snagged up—you've been fishing with a hook that has no barb."

As they walked back, hand in hand, Corey was laughing. "I'm glad I found these berries. I hate to go home 'skunked,' as Pa used to say. It's strange"—she was remembering that day he'd left—"I never thought to find anyone again who'd take me fishing."

Ethan didn't smile. His sensitive face was serious as he said, "It's not many a girl who knows how to be a man's friend."

The words worked on Corey, ringing some other, older echoes—of Sister Trude's salty soup and Millie's recipe for being lovable and foolish. And the doctor's warning to her that Ethan would need something more. It came over Corey that this might even be what he meant.

It seemed too short a time until they reached the Fort again.

"I wonder what's afoot?" Ethan said, puzzled.

Around the Mormon encampment people were milling excitedly. Down near their own wagon Lucy was standing bareheaded in the cool afternoon breeze, talking to a little group of women. When she saw them she came running, her long face luminous.

"News! Wonderful, wonderful news! Just imagine—they've found the promised land! A rider's come in only a few minutes ago. Brother Brigham and the advance party have come through the mountains into Zion!"

It sounded almost too good to believe when the details were all told: A fair valley with fresh running rivers and a great lake whose margins would supply enough salt and saleratus to last them forever. Green meadows and plenty of game and good soil, a land of great richness, just as the Lord had promised His children.

"What's more, it's off the Oregon trail," Dan said with grim satisfaction. "Won't be any temptation for any Missourian to wander through ever. There's mountains all around. Everybody down on your knees this minute; we'll thank the Lord for them mountains."

Corey tried to be properly grateful, but even as she bowed her head along with the rest of the family she was fingering a folded sheet of paper in her pocket. The same rider who had brought this larger news had borne messages from those ahead and even a few long-delayed letters from the Battalion, far out in California somewhere. For the first time in a year Corey had word from her father.

As soon as the prayer was over and Dan had given them his blessing, they dispersed to their own wagons. Once alone Corey lit the candle beside her bunk and reread the words that Pa had spelled out so carefully:

> They say this war's near over, and a foolish one it has seemed to me, Corey. There was no virtue in it, but short rations for us all. We've come clean to California without a battle, praise God, and soon my duty will be over. I find this country well favored and may stay a while. I wish you were here with me, for I've had much uneasiness over you.
>
> It was a misfortune we had to act so hasty before I left. I see it more now–it is not for another to look into your heart, and while I don't doubt that Ethan is a good man, yet I fear you may not come to feel as a wife should. This is on my mind often now, since I have made acquaintance with a fine woman in this territory and hope to wed with her. She is of our faith, Corey; she came to this coast on the ship, *Brooklyn*, which sailed clean around the bottom of the world to bring the Saints to this coast. But there is some Church counsel which neither she nor I can hold with, and it is of this I must speak.
>
> I hope I am a God-fearing man, but this year I've seen many things and thought a lot. I believe now it is not meant for a man to take more than one wife. I will not do it, and I like not the thought that you may have to share a man's affection with sundry others. Of this

you must decide yourself, but I give you my leave to choose your own way.

You are near of age now and can take care of yourself, I reckon. If you want to come to me, I advise you join a gentile train traveling west. I have found these people are not all scoundrels. I will leave word for you at Sutter's Fort and will stop there, now and again, if you wish to write your loving father,

Respectfully,

Judd T.

With a fond smile, Corey blew out the lamp and lay back, breathing a silent, shivery, little thanks. One thing, at least, which had been troubling her was at an end. If a certain day were ever to come out of all this—that day she was praying for—she thought that Ethan and Pa were going to like each other.

Nineteen

They took the trail again that next morning in a blaze of anticipation. As one group after another rolled out, people were singing, calling to each other with new zest. The camp rang with bustle and turmoil until Sister Elizabeth put her hands over her ears.

"Why do we have to go on?" she asked plaintively. "This seems a pleasant place. I—I'd really like another trout."

Ethan kissed her lightly. "There'll be better brooks than this in the promised land."

But she hardly seemed to know what he was talking about. When the wagon rolled out, she huddled down in her pillows, disheartened. Corey tucked her in, then went to join Ethan, trying to hide her discouragement. After seeing Sister Elizabeth eat the fish with such relish she had hoped, in spite of everything, it boded well.

Now she tried to speak lightly.

"Do you think we might give your mother a sleeping powder?"

Ethan cracked the whip over the oxen. "I gave her the last I had weeks ago."

They had hardly left the Fort behind when the pitch of the land began to grow much steeper than before. The trail was rocky and uneven—time after time Ethan had to give Corey the whip and go back to set a shoulder against the wheel, throwing his strength behind the heaving oxen, to wrench the wagon out of some chuckhole. It was as she drove the team that Corey noticed how her hand was still aching where she had stabbed it with the fishhook. She had dismissed it at the time—the puncture was such a slight one, it had hardly even bled.

And yet in the next few days the pain continued to grow sharper and a redness was spreading. At night she would waken in the darkness to feel her whole palm pulsing, though by morning, with so much to do, she pitched into her work in spite of the pain.

They were pushing ahead at an unrelenting pace now. They had left the Platte, where it took a bend into a steep canyon, and followed the trail out across a dry alkali waste. On this high tableland the gusty wind blew out of the west day and night, raising the dust that the wheels ground up, driving it into squinted eyes where it burned like raw salt.

On every side were the scattered bones of oxen,

splintered bits of wagons and odds and ends of furniture, discarded possessions that had once been someone's valuables. They spelled out a story of panic, pitiful haste to rush through this fearful stretch. Even the Saints, for all their discipline, began to grow frightened, when each time they reached water it turned out to be poisonous. It was all the captains could do to keep them calm and make sure the dwindling contents of the casks were portioned out judiciously to the oxen.

At the noonday stop Corey always helped Ethan water the team, though she was finding the bucket hard to manage, with one hand scarcely able to grip it. In fact, the second day out in the heart of this blinding wasteland, with the sun blazing down, a sudden dizziness came over her, black spots swarmed before her eyes and she had to set the pail down quickly.

Ethan hurried to her side.

"Nothing," she laughed breathlessly as she clung to him. "Just this hand of mine—it gave me a twinge." She held it out accusingly. The fingers were puffed up like risen dough and dark red streaks had begun to reach forth from the inflamed center.

As Ethan stared at it the blood drained from his face, leaving it ashen under the tan. "How long—?" he stammered. "How— What caused this?"

"It happened that day we went fishing." She told him of the accident. "I've been thinking if the barb broke off in there I ought to try to dig it out."

Ethan shook his head sharply, unable to hide his concern. "It's too late for that now. The infection is spread all through the tissues. To open it might disperse the poison into your blood stream and that–" He broke off, his breath coming short. "No, we've got to try to concentrate it first. Wait–" He climbed into the wagon and came back hurriedly with a scrap of clean toweling. "Here, wet this–no, get water from the cask on the other side of the wagon. The sun's been on it all morning, it should be warm. Keep the cloth moistened and pressed to your hand as we go along."

"And then what?" she asked. The pain in her hand seemed less important than the consternation which still lingered in his face, some terrible emotion which she thought must spring from some reason he wasn't telling. "When it gathers, then what?"

"We'll see," he said grimly. "The scouts report that there are gentile trains just ahead of us. We'll come in sight of them when we reach the next river valley. At least we'll be close enough that I can go in search of a doctor."

To the parched travelers who stumbled wearily down off the dusty flat into the green meadows beside the Sweetwater, a river had never been better named. Small, beautiful, shallow enough to ford easily, it meandered down from the far-off mountains to the west. At every bend there could be seen smoke from other encampments–pilgrims, sainted and unsaintly, willing to forget their suspicions to share the blessing of clear, cold water.

The train camped in the shadow of a huge turtle-backed rock which was said to be called "Independence Rock"—a place where other grateful emigrants had paused and chipped their names in the stone. As soon as supper was over, a time of rejoicing was declared and Shad began to tune his fiddle while the others collected around him to dance.

Corey felt a long way off from them as she walked alone down by the riverbank, but she couldn't regret it. The only thing that really mattered was Ethan, out there alone somewhere in the darkening evening. Gone to look for help—for her.

These past two days he had worked stubbornly and painstakingly to cause the infection to draw back. Each night he had made her soak her hand in hot salt water for hours. And slowly the red streaks had receded, the swelling gone down enough that he said it could be opened if it were done carefully. She had asked him to do it himself, but he had cut her short with a nervous refusal and gone off into the dusk, heading upriver toward the gentile camps.

As night drew on, Corey knew she should return to Sister Elizabeth, even though after supper she seldom wakened. And yet there was a temptation to linger and watch for him. At last she caught a slight sound, of someone splashing across the river just above, and the familiar long-legged figure came striding down to her through the darkness.

Corey hurried to meet him. Even in the dim light of the stars she could see that he was upset. "There isn't a doctor on the trail this side of Sutter's Fort, so far as anyone knows. I'd not dreamed it was this bad. What do they all do when some illness or accident occurs?"

"Just what we always did," she said matter-of-factly. "Pa and me. I've seen him dig for a splinter a hundred times. I reckon I can get the barb out myself." She was starting back toward the wagon when he caught her and swung her around to face him.

"Corey, listen to me. It's no job for a novice. It was from just such a thing as this that my father died." The words were torn out of him so harshly that she halted in her tracks. Slowly he went on. "He'd got an infection of the foot and called in a friend of his—another doctor—to care for it. A good man, but when he opened it something went wrong, the infection spread. Blood poisoning set in. There was only one choice—to amputate the leg. Not everyone can stand such a thing—no way on earth to blunt that kind of agony. My father died on the operating table. I was there—" He couldn't go on.

"And that's why"—she hardly knew she spoke aloud —"that's why you gave it all up. You're worried you'll make a mistake—you can't bear to hurt anyone—"

Ethan took her arm and led the way through the darkness. When they reached the wagon he went in ahead of her, got the lantern lit. He seemed to be under only a thin, uncertain control as he went about setting candles in the small stove and put a pan of water on to heat. While Corey watched he went to unlock his chest of medicines, taking out a gleaming little knife, a probe, and some thin forceps. When the water began to simmer, he dropped them into it. Into his knapsack he put a roll of lint and some clean strips of bandage, took a flask from his pocket.

"I've used up most of my surgical supplies—all my cauterizers are exhausted. But I managed just now to buy some whisky from a bullwhacker up the river." He glanced at her nervously. "I suppose I knew what I was going to do."

Corey smiled at him warmly, with all the love she had. If she could only ease that tightness in him—but the veins stood out on his forehead as he finished his preparations.

"We'll not do it here—I don't want to be interrupted." He wrapped the instruments in lint and put them in his pocket. "Bring the lantern but don't light it yet. I think the moon will be up."

It hadn't quite cleared the horizon as he helped her down out of the wagon, but the whole eastern sky was silvering. There was enough light to let them make their way toward the looming bulk of the big rock, skirting it stealthily until they had left the squeal of the fiddle and the fires of camp far behind. Clear around to the far side Ethan took her, then lighting the lantern spread out his instruments on a piece of towel and motioned her to sit down opposite him.

Knee to knee they sat, bent over the festered hand—Ethan seemed to take a long time studying it. Then, pouring some whisky onto a cloth, he bathed the swollen area with the strong-smelling stuff.

A little shaky herself, Corey tried to joke it away. "I trust the Devil won't object to see his brew put to good use for once."

Ethan didn't seem to hear. He was fingering the delicate knife. Even though the sighing night wind was cool, his brow gleamed moist in the lantern light and his hands were trembling. Hesitantly he glanced at her. Corey looked away, off into the velvet night sky.

"Go ahead," she said carelessly.

It was a long, long moment before she felt the knife bite. Her belly muscles jerked tight, but she held still and didn't murmur as he went cautiously deeper. Each small cut sent a needle-sharp pain shooting up through her arm. She glanced sidelong at Ethan. But now the fear had smoothed out of his face, leaving it composed, intent—he was moving as decisively as he always had, those times in the past when he had come to grips with this strange art. With the delicacy of a fine craftsman he extracted something with the forceps and held it up so that it glinted in the light.

"You've found it!" she gasped with relief.

Ethan looked up at her with grim satisfaction, then as he saw something beyond, his face tightened. Another light was bobbing toward them.

"We'd better put these things away," she whispered.

"Can't—not yet. It's got to be cauterized." Swiftly he tipped the bottle of liquor and doused her hand liberally. Corey hardly felt the sting of it in the panic that struck her as she recognized Dan's bearded face in the upward cast of the oncoming light. As he came up a terrible rage transfixed his features.

"When I found you gone I had a notion you were at some ungodly work again!"

Ethan didn't glance up, but went on fashioning a bandage. "Nothing sinful about taking out a splinter, is there, Dan?"

Tanner glared at the bloody instruments and cloths; his eye fell on the flask, which was plainly marked "whisky," and a choking roar burst from him.

"You've fuddled this innocent child with liquor!"

He started forward. Ethan made a quick move, yanked the double-barreled pistol from beneath his shirt, and leveled it. His hand was steady as rock.

"Don't come any nearer. I'd dislike to shoot you, Dan."

Tanner halted, stunned. There could be no doubt that Ethan meant it. "Daughter—!" he began.

"She'll stay here until I give her leave to go." Calmly Ethan motioned with the gun. "Sit still, Corey."

"You'll regret this," Tanner said furiously. "I'll have the men out—we'll take you! You'll stand trial as a wilful sinner."

Ethan shook his head. "No need to raise the whole camp. I'll be gone before you could get back."

"Go, then! You've never been one of us!" Dan snapped. "But the girl's ours. She's too young to know what she's doing. You shan't have her."

"She'll be back with you in ten minutes. Now leave us."

As Tanner strode away from them, Ethan took the bottle of liquor and once more drenched the open wound, then set about dressing it rapidly. "You must keep it clean at all costs. And keep putting hot packs on it until the redness is entirely gone."

But Corey was too shaken to listen. "Where will you go? Ethan—what of your mother?"

"For her sake, I've tried to avoid this," he said evenly. "God knows I've tried. But I've seen this coming. There arrives a time when patience is no longer a virtue. Will you take care of her? I know it's a great deal to ask."

"Of course! But what of you?"

"I won't be far away. I'll wait and try to find work with the next gentile train along—I don't want to travel ahead of you. At night I'll find some way to slip into camp and see her, though not for the present. Not unless it's an emergency."

"Be careful!" she breathed. "Dan means it—they could really have you up for treason against the Church."

"Don't think of that." He helped her to her feet. "Especially don't think of it if you need me urgently. If your hand doesn't improve at once, or if Mother takes a turn for the worse, put out two candles. After the others have gone to bed, set them facing the back

trail and I'll be on watch. Two candles, and I'll come."
Before she knew what he was about, he had kissed her, a swift, tender embrace. "I had to do that–once."

And then he was lost in the darkness.

Twenty

The Elder who was their captain sat hunched over his writing desk, eying Corey, as dour as a judge. He was a short, stocky man with grizzled hair and bleak blue eyes. His face was sallow, as if he, too, had been assailed by the mountain sickness that was bringing down so many.

To Dan he said, "The girl's father entrusted her to you? You made a covenant with him, to protect her and guide her?"

"That's so, Brother." Dan mopped his brow. It was hot in the tent.

No, Corey denied silently. *Pa's trusted me to choose my own way*. She thought of bringing out his letter to prove it, but held the impulse in check, forcing herself to think of Sister Elizabeth. This was no time to take a chance on being turned out of the train.

"And now the girl refuses to obey you?"

"Forgive her, Brother," Dan said sorrowfully. "She's not any foolisher than most females, but the boy's laid a spell over her. I take the full blame for it—I've known for quite a while that he was unworthy, but I kept hoping we could lead him to salvation. I'm bitter ashamed I wasn't able."

The Elder stroked his chin. "He's deserted the Church, you say?"

"He has. And I've dissolved the vows I spoke over 'em, only the lass doesn't seem to rejoice in it yet. She used to be a fine, obedient girl." Dan's hand fell on Corey's shoulder with bear-like affection. "I'm praying for her, Elder, but she needs to be settled with another mate. That'll get her over the megrims quicker than anything."

"Please!" Corey protested, with the sinking feeling that it was useless. "How can anyone except my own pa say who I must wed?"

"Your father chose ye a family," Dan admonished her. "It weren't his fault we harbored a sinner. But I aim to make up for it." To the Elder he went on, "My boy, Shad, has favor with the Church beyond his years. The Council gave him leave to take a wife in Winter Quarters. He's willing to accept the care of a second, even such a poor, bedeviled girl as this, and try to bring her to salvation, if you say so, Brother."

The Elder twiddled his quill pen. "Ask your son to come in."

Dan went to the open tent flap and called. A moment later Shad strode in—a powerful figure, his beard nearly as long as Dan's now, his bare arms bronzed and muscular. The old light of daring was in the glance he tossed Corey, but it was the look of a man—no longer the brash impudence of a boy. When he turned to the Elder, he was all respect.

The old man studied him thoughtfully. "Why do you seek a second wife, son?"

Shad seemed shocked. "I don't, sir! Seeing as how my first is carrying a child, and I've but one wagon, if I take on the duties of a second it'll be mortal hard to manage for a while. Besides, this young female has always been wayward and unladylike, wearing men's clothes and prancing 'round the woods alone. I swear, she's been a trial to us all. No, sir, I don't especially *crave* to wed her, but I feel 'tis my duty."

The answer seemed to impress the Elder, but he spoke a word of warning. "You know that lust is a sin, and that your wedding with this girl will be for the sake of her spirit."

"Absolutely, sir." Shad looked pained.

"Then I so order it." The Elder dismissed them with a wave of his hand.

Corey swallowed down a whole flood of argument. She could see that it would do no good. Bitterly she remembered Ethan's brooding remark about some things being too personal to be ordered by others, no matter how wise.

"Sir," she said, forcing herself to sound submissive, "I'll do what I must, but my father was set against my being sealed before I turned sixteen, and that's over a month off yet."

Dan started to protest, but the Elder cut him short. "It's a reasonable condition. So be it."

As the three of them walked away from the tent, Dan was sober. "It would stick in my craw to speak more vows, after the sorry time we've all had over the last ones. We'll just consider the betrothal made." He glanced down at Corey, his big, honest face contorted with remorse. "Things will be better from now on, daughter. I promise you." To Shad he added sternly, "As for you, son, I heard a mite of over-righteousness in your tone, back there when you were speaking to the Elder. I advise you, pray for humility."

"I will," Shad said gravely. "I will."

As Dan went back to his own wagon, Corey had turned to go in to Sister Elizabeth when Shad laid a hand on her arm—lightly, but with a proprietary touch.

"I don't mind waiting a few more weeks," he said with a flicker of amusement beneath his soberness. "Give you time to get in the true spirit of cooperation, which I don't reckon you are right now. Thought you were too good to be my first wife, so now you'll have to take the second seat. Come to think of it, I judge you may just have to stand back from the table entirely and wait till Meg and me are through before you eat—humility, you know—that's a virtue, Sister Corey."

She stood coolly, waiting for him to release her. It seemed to anger Shad. Glancing around—they were hidden by the wagon from the rest of the camp—he jerked her to him and would have kissed her if she hadn't turned her head away quickly, with such distaste that he reddened furiously.

"There'll come a day soon when you won't have the right to deny me—anything. I'll bring you down off that high horse, so help me! You'll learn!"

With tight-clasped hands Corey made herself sit still and watch the sun set slowly behind a bank of clouds in the west. A while ago she had tried to get Sister Elizabeth to eat a little bread and milk but had hardly got a bite down her. Now she was asleep, and Corey sat, too tense inside to want supper herself. She could hear the others gathered around the fires, their voices rising in an indistinct babble. For the first time that whole year Corey hadn't gone to help with the common chores. She'd half expected Dan to come and chastise her, but they'd all left her alone.

Little by little the big, quiet country around worked to ease the strain on her nerves. They were camped on a long slope near a spring—a whole meadow of springs—from which a stream of clear water spilled, running west. All this past week they had climbed the sage prairies until that morning they had crossed a rolling swell in the land and found themselves on a downhill pitch. Here was the first western water—Pacific Springs, they called it, though it was a far stretch of imagination to picture it finding its way to the ocean out where Pa was.

For a moment Corey's thoughts went out to him fleetingly; then reached backward to those other trains which they had lost to sight as they crossed the divide. Tonight she was afraid that Ethan must still be far behind somewhere on the Sweetwater. Too far to come —a twinge gripped her. All these days there had been no sign of him. She had tried to be patient, but tonight the longing was keen as a sharp edge inside her.

As darkness drew on she took out two candles and set them in the lantern, ready. And yet she had to wait —endlessly. It was hours before the camp quieted into full sleep. At last she dared light them and set them on the tailgate of the wagon, crouched just inside, ready to blow them out if she heard anyone coming.

The minutes stretched out like a string drawn tighter and tighter. Behind her in the wagon she heard Sister Elizabeth stir and murmur restlessly, and went to soothe her. As she straightened, she heard the least small sound outside, then Ethan ducked in under the canvas, bringing the lantern with him.

In a rush she was in his arms—wordlessly they held each other with an aching fierceness. At last he loosened his clasp a little and looked down at her, stroking her hair.

"I've been near beside myself, worrying." And for sure he looked as if he had slept little.

"So have I—I've imagined a million awful things—"

"About me? No need. I'm traveling with a gentile train not far behind you. They've been kind to me, gave me my keep for a few chores and even loaned me a horse, to ride forward these nights and look for the signal. I wanted to come find you, but I was afraid it would make things harder on you if they'd posted a guard."

"No, there's been no watch set, but I've been afraid to summon you for fear what Dan might do if he caught you. Until tonight—I had to see you."

"Is Mother worse?" He glanced over anxiously.

"She's getting more vague all the time. I told her you had to be away—she thinks you're in Scotland, hunting."

He shook his head hopelessly. "Let me see your hand."

"It's almost healed. I don't even feel it." She held it out to show him. "That night after you left I hid the instruments. Dan came searching for them, but I told him you took them. He broke all the bottles, though."

Ethan was still examining her hand. He didn't answer at once. Sister Elizabeth roused again and he went to her side. When she saw him she gave a little moan of relief and struggled to sit up.

"You've been away so long—"

"Softly, now. We don't want to wake the whole household, do we?" He sat down beside her.

"Did Dr. Drake return with you?" she asked wistfully.

"No, Father's still in the Highlands. I'm going up

there again myself, shortly." For a while he talked to her, while Corey kept watch at the rear flap of the wagon. It wasn't long, though, until Sister Elizabeth grew drowsy again and slipped off to sleep, even while he was speaking. Folding the coverlet around her shoulders, he turned away.

"I should come oftener," he said. "Have they been hard on you?"

"All week I've been lectured and prayed over and now, today, it's been ordered that I must wed with Shad next month." She tried not to sound upset, but she saw a slow-burning anger start in his face. "That's why I wanted to see you tonight," she went on a little breathlessly. "I can't stay here—not with these folk, forever. Even Pa says I must choose, myself, about who to love. He wrote me to act as I see fit, and I've decided. Ethan, I'm ready to go with you, and no regret."

Ethan put his hands on her shoulders, lightly, as if to reassure himself. "I've been hoping you would say this. It means I must think what to do. I've been trying to decide—" He broke off, listening.

Corey held her breath. There was a light sound, a faint tap at the tailgate of the wagon. Stooping swiftly, Ethan blew out the candles, then Corey went to lift the flap. The stars were brilliant across the sky. Under the sheen of light she saw Sister Trude, standing bareheaded, the heavy gray hair loose about her shoulders, a cloak clutched over her nightclothes.

"Dan just got up," she said in a low voice. "If those candles of yours happened to fetch a visitor, it's time he went his way." And before Corey could answer, the shadowy figure was moving back across the camp.

Ethan was at her side now. "Thank Sister for me," he said hurriedly. "I'd not have thought she'd do me a favor. In two nights light the candles again when everyone's abed—that way I can find the wagon quickly."

"Wait! Your instruments—don't you want to take them?"

He swung down to the ground. As he started off, she caught the hushed, uneasy words. ". . . to be thought about."

Twenty-one

The days of the calendar took on an ominous meaning now, as Corey crossed them off one by one. Shad was watching them, too. Though he didn't even try to catch her alone again, there was anticipation in his whole bearing as he drove Sister Elizabeth's wagon. Dan was seeing to it that Shad felt the burden of his new responsibility; he himself drove Shad's team part of each day so that the boy could help Corey with hers.

She stayed inside during those hours, holding Sister Elizabeth's hands, trying to distract her attention from the swaying of the wagon. These hot August days they made their way across a merciless stretch of desert, where false images shimmered in the blinding sun. A single thread of water led them a tortuous trail, day after day, until it seemed as though they were caught on a treadmill. And in the distance rose the thin blue line of ragged mountains—the Wasatch—into which the Mormons would venture alone, leaving the main trail behind. It was beyond those peaks that Brigham Young had discovered their valley. But the crossing was said to be perilously steep.

Sitting beside Sister Elizabeth, Corey sometimes looked at the frail body and grieved to think what was ahead. Almost worse was her anxiety for Ethan. She kept wondering how he would live, once he had to leave the gentile train he was traveling with, yet couldn't risk joining a Mormon party. He himself wouldn't discuss it. The nights when he came and they sat together whispering in the darkness she had put the question to him more than once. All he would say was, "I'll do as best I can to stay near you."

"At least take Peggy," she begged.

"No, they'd suspect something and keep a closer watch. Besides, if anything delays me and I'm not near when your birth date comes you may need the mare, yourself, to escape."

"I'm going to try to put them off," she said. "I won't leave your mother."

His arms tightened around her gratefully. "You've done all you could. She would feel the same: you mustn't sacrifice yourself too far."

Corey kept her own counsel as to that. In her heart she knew she'd not be able to forsake the little Englishwoman—the only mother she had ever known. But secretly she had to admit she had no plan to delay the marriage much beyond the appointed date.

And then at last they neared the point where the trail would divide—Fort Bridger. Here the few remaining California and Oregon trains, those which hadn't already taken the cutoff, would veer northward on a long sweep that would take them around the mountains. It was a beautiful spot—this last outpost. Jim Bridger, the old mountain man, had built his fort in a green valley, an oasis to the pilgrims who had just crossed the long, terrible stretch of dry land.

When the wagons had formed their circles near the cluster of log buildings, the weary, dust-caked Saints stumbled gratefully over to sink down beside the cold little stream that forked its way across the broad meadows. Under the welcome shade of huge cottonwoods the Elder gave his blessing and told them to rest for a day and thank the Lord. Corey had a notion that most people were more concerned with prayers of supplication, since the few "tens" who were ahead of them had sent back word that from here on the climb was mortal hard.

Only one person seemed not to be giving the trials of the crossing much thought, and that was Meg. These evenings when they all were gathered around the common table, she looked so wretched with jealousy that Corey pitied her, in spite of the venomous glances Meg tossed her way. She wished she could assure the girl that she wanted no part of Shad, but knew it would only make matters worse. The sorry part was that someday Meg might have to share him with three or four others. A man such as Shad was not likely to consider it a burden.

More and more with each passing day Corey was sure she was justified in planning to rebel against her fate, but she missed the few precious midnight moments when Ethan had held her and steadied her. She knew, of course, that he couldn't come into the grounds of the Fort without being seen, but once their train had left the valley, grinding westward up the newly broken trail, she set the candles out every night. And still he didn't come.

They were in a tremendous canyon now, a corridor of sheer red rock that took them deeper and deeper into this fearsome range. The trail was crude in places, hacked out of solid rock—it jolted and racked the wagon worse than ever, until by evening Sister Elizabeth was exhausted and dazed. And always cold. A haze of autumn lay over the heights now, and every night a layer of ice formed on the water pails. Through the long, chill hours Corey crouched beside her lantern, watching until the candles burned out. What sleep she got was only fitful. And come morning, she was almost afraid to go to the little invalid for fear the thin thread of life might have parted during the night.

Ethan must realize what's happening! she told herself desperately. *If he could come, he would.* But that thought hardly comforted her as the days passed.

There was a cruel beauty about these Wasatch Mountains, thicketed with dense scrub oak and aspen, turning red and yellow now. They were a maze of canyons that twisted and turned, disappearing or growing too precipitous to climb. It seemed incredible that the scouts had found a way through them at all. Even so, as they reached the upper grades the teams had to be doubled and tripled, inching upward with one wagon for a mile or two, then going back for another.

Everyone able to walk was ordered to go afoot, and so it was that Corey was trudging along the trail beside the wagon when she heard the cry go up ahead. The first climbers had topped the summit and stood looking out westward, shading their eyes, turning to pound each other jubilantly. The men blocked the wheels of the wagons and left the animals to blow, while they rushed ahead themselves, Corey and the women following after.

It was a dizzying sight. Ahead of them the mountains fell away in a ruinous descent; beyond was the great valley, bounded on the south by high peaks; there were others to the west, faint in the distance; and still more to the north, to complete a fierce barrier that isolated the tableland below. A gray immense land. Off to the west a huge lake glittered in the sun, its shores brilliant white—the lake of salt water that the couriers had mentioned.

"There she is, the land of milk and honey," one man whispered to another. To Corey it looked terribly empty. Glancing around, she glimpsed the same dismay shadowed in the faces of the other women, though when the hymn of thanks was struck up, they joined in sturdily.

"By the Lord, Sister Elizabeth must see this!" Dan turned to go back to the wagon. "I'll fetch her."

"Sir!" Corey blurted out anxiously "I doubt she could stand the excitement. She's dreadful weak."

"Of course she can!" he roared jubilantly. "The Lord will strengthen her. She'll be healed just by the sight of Zion!" He came back in a few moments, carrying the little Englishwoman as easily as he would a child. And miraculously Sister Elizabeth did seem suddenly restored to her native bright awareness—far more clearheaded than Corey had seen her in weeks. She smiled around at them, and when Dan held her up to see the country stretched before them, she clasped her hands in rapture.

"There it is, Sister—what we've all come so far to find!" Dan was swelling with emotion. He towered among them, a giant patriarch.

With her eyes fixed on the white, barren sands of the salt flats beyond the lake, Sister Elizabeth cried, "It's beautiful! More beautiful than I ever dreamed. All those fruit groves—and the rose gardens and fountains—"

The others looked at her uneasily, but Dan was beaming with faith. "And so it will be! So it will be!"

All through supper that evening Sister Elizabeth was

agitated and happy. For once she seemed completely aware of where she was and, oddly, Ethan's absence didn't appear to worry her.

"He's much like his father," she confided to Corey. "They must have some time alone, to think. Don't fret, my dear, he'll be along soon. Won't he be glad that we've come in sight of our home at last?"

It was difficult to get her to go to bed, but at last she sighed and quieted down, sinking off to sleep. Corey hardly waited for the last noises of the camp to die before she set the candles out again. For hours they burned, until finally one guttered out as its wick tumbled into the wax. Almost to the point of desperation, Corey went to get another—they were kept in a box under Sister Elizabeth's bunk.

As she bent over to get it, something struck her as strange—a stillness. She couldn't even catch the sound of shallow breathing. Frantically she ran back to get the lighted candle and held it high. But it took only a glance to know that the face nestled in the pillows had settled into its last, faint, lovely smile.

Twenty-two

Sister Trude stood looking down at the quiet figure in the bunk. "I'm thankful, for her sake," she said at last. "I've a notion that bitter, hard times are ahead for the rest of us."

For all her own grief, Corey knew that it was true—there could be no regret over the tranquillity of that sleep which had, once and for all, smoothed the lines from Sister Elizabeth's face. She realized that her sharpest heartache was for Ethan. . . .

"The boy hasn't been here for some nights, has he?" Trude asked keenly.

Corey shivered. "Not since before we reached Bridger. I'm afraid what may have happened to him."

"What will you do?" The older woman put the question to her so straightly, Corey had to answer it in kind.

"Try to find him. As soon as she's laid to rest—"

"Nonsense. The rest of us will see to that. Every minute you stay here will make it harder for you to get away. Dan can be almighty set on a thing when he feels it's his duty. You must leave tonight."

Corey stared at her wonderingly. "You'll help me?"

"If you don't dawdle." Sister Trude tried to sound brusque. "Get those man clothes of yours on, and be quiet about it. Don't leave the wagon, though, until I tell you all's clear." Nightgown flapping, slippers scuffing she went out.

Left alone, Corey hesitated a moment longer, but she had to admit it made sense to slip away now. She thought Ethan would say the same. Fumbling and frightened, feeling terribly alone, she went about changing her clothes, bundling up his surgical instruments along with her own few belongings. When she packed the blue velvet dress which Sister Elizabeth had helped her make so long ago, the ache in her throat grew almost unbearable.

It seemed a long while before Sister Trude came back. She was carrying an oilskin packet. "You'll need food as you go along."

Numbly Corey took it. "I've done nothing to deserve your kindness."

"Does there have to be a reason? Maybe I'm beholden to the boy—Lucy told me what happened to her back there in 'Misery Bottoms' last winter. As for you—well, say you remind me of somebody." Suddenly the tough, worn old face was full of compassion.

"You're more like me than either one of my own girls. Wilful, and so was I. Went my own way, took up a faith my folks were set against. Married a man for love. He's over there now—in another wagon. I learned to take that calm, but I don't know as I'd wish it on you." She shrugged impatiently. "Don't ask me any more questions, but get on your way. And God be with you, child."

Standing alone in the first frigid gray of dawn, Corey felt the grip of panic. In a moment more it would be all finished—everything she had grown up with. Out of old habit she whispered certain familiar words, half expecting them to sound hollow inside her. Instead, they brought the same sense of comfort as always, and she knew that nothing was really changed too much. Steadied, she made her way to the herd—Peggy came to her readily, and she slipped on the bridle. Leading the horse quietly away from camp, she looked back once at the shadowy circle of wagons, with a last silent rush of affection for the sleepers there. Then scrambling to the mare's back, she dug in her heels.

It was tricky going, down the steep back trail. Urging Peggy over the rocky descent as fast as she dared, Corey tried not to think of how she might pass Ethan, if he had taken some short cut on foot across the hogback ridges; she told herself he wouldn't have risked missing her, knowing that she might soon be backtracking, herself.

Once they had reached the more level ground in the

canyon bottoms, she let the mare stretch out into a long lope that ate up the miles. But as she passed company after company of Saints with no sign of him, her heart began to sink.

Afterward she hardly remembered where she slept that night—somewhere in the red-rock canyon. Curled up in the shelter of a draw she waited out the hours while the mare rested and grazed, and the stars climbed the sky and started down again. At daylight she was on her way, the hasty meal she had eaten lumped like a brick inside her. She didn't go so wide of the trains now, but pounded past while the families stared after her curiously.

Then a long hill—she remembered this. Bridger's Fort was at the foot. But what then? To wait? Or keep going? Not tonight. Darkness was coming on fast. Far below in the valley the scatter of lights was almost lost under the deepening pall of dusk.

A few minutes later, as she rode across the big meadow, she saw that there weren't so many trains now camped around the fort; what few were there, seemed to be Mormons. She could hear the rise of hymns from one camp, the murmur of prayers coming from another. Slowing Peggy to a walk, she made her way among them and over toward the log buildings in the center of the campground.

Two old men lounged in the open gate of the fort, gabbing idly—by their profanity she judged they were no saints. Glad that the darkness concealed her appearance somewhat, she slid down off the mare's back and went over to them.

"Evenin', laddie," one greeted her. "Seen you ride in. Ain't many folks coming from the west these days."

"I have a message for someone—" Corey's voice was hoarse with fatigue. "A man—he's probably with one of the gentile trains."

"Gentile?" The other puffed on his pipe and a red glow lit his face for an instant. "That's Mormon talk. You one of them?"

"N-no, sir," she faltered, as the truth of it struck home.

"Well, there ain't no other parties here now. The Californy trains have all gone on. Any outfit that ain't got here by now would be too late to make it clear on to the coast before snow. I doubt we'll have another bunch through this year. Reckon you've missed him."

"He—wouldn't have gone on." Sickly Corey started to turn away.

"Come to think of it, you might inquire about him of them folks in the tent down yonder. They was with a Californy outfit, but had to drop out, Missus give birth—like to have died. For over a week now they gave her up, and the baby, too. But that young doctor brought 'em through—"

Corey didn't wait to hear more—she was running for the tent. Its open door made a triangle of light at the far end of the meadow. And then she stopped, just short of the lantern glow. Inside on a cot lay a woman; a man sat beside her, an awkward, gangling young fellow who held one of her hands in both his rough ones.

On the opposite side of the tent stood Ethan, holding in the crook of one arm a bundle from which two small red fists waved angrily and a feeble cry rose. As Corey watched he stooped to pick up a makeshift nursing bottle which had been heating in a pan of water on the stove and offered it to his young patient. The crying stopped. Ethan smiled with weary satisfaction; he was in shirt sleeves, his hair was tousled, and there were lines of stress about his mouth and eyes. But his face had the look of peace of a man who has come to terms with himself.

Out in the darkness Corey was trembling with relief. Because it was going to be all right. In a minute she would go in to him and a whole new world would begin. In just a minute . . .